house of stairs

house of stairs

WILLIAM SLEATOR

PUFFIN BOOKS

PUFFIN BOOKS
Published by the Penguin Group
Penguin Books USA Inc.,
375 Hudson Street, New York, New York 10014, U.S.A.
Penguin Books Ltd, 27 Wrights Lane, London W8 5TZ, England
Penguin Books Australia Ltd, Ringwood, Victoria, Australia
Penguin Books Canada Ltd, 10 Alcorn Avenue, Toronto, Ontario, Canada M4V 3B2
Penguin Books (N.Z.) Ltd, 182–190 Wairau Road, Auckland 10, New Zealand

Penguin Books Ltd, Registered Offices: Harmondsworth, Middlesex, England

First published in the United States of America by E. P. Dutton, 1974
Published in Puffin Books, 1991
3 5 7 9 10 8 6 4 2
Copyright © William Sleator, 1974
All rights reserved

LIBRARY OF CONGRESS CATALOGING IN PUBLICATION DATA
Sleator, William   House of stairs / William Sleator.   p. cm.
Summary: Five sixteen-year-old orphans of widely varying
personality characteristics are involuntarily placed in a house of
endless stairs as subjects for a psychological experiment on
conditioned human response.
ISBN: 0-14-034580-9
[1. Science fiction.] I. Title.
PZ7.S6313Ho 1991   [Fic]—dc20   90-41419

Printed in the United States of America
Set in Caledonia

*This book is dedicated to
all the rats and pigeons
who have already been here*

part one

chapter 1

The whirring around them had been going on for quite a long time. It sounded as though they were in an elevator, but the movement was so smooth that he could not tell whether they were being carried up or down or even to the side. Once again, as they had done several times in the past hour, his hands moved involuntarily to reach up and push the blindfold away from his eyes; and once again they were stopped by the cord that bound his wrists. But he did not struggle against the cord. Peter never struggled.

After a time the whirring stopped. The cord was removed, and he was pushed gently forward. Quick, efficient hands untied his blindfold and pulled it off. The door behind him slid shut, the whirring began, faded away, and he was alone.

For a moment he could not see, quickly closing his eyes against the white glare. He closed them again just as quickly, suddenly dizzy, after his first clear look at where he was. It was very cautiously that he opened them for the third time.

All he could see were stairs. The high, narrow landing on which he stood seemed to be the only flat place there was, and above and below him, growing smaller in the distance, were only flights of steps. Without railings they rose and fell at alarming angles, forking, occasionally spiraling, rising briefly together only to veer apart again, crossing above and below one another, connected at rare intervals by thin bridges spanning deep gulfs. Nothing supported them; the glossy white material from which they were made seemed to be strong enough to arch alone across great distances. They were not outdoors, the all-pervasive yet indirect glare came from artificial light, but he could see no walls, floor, or ceiling. Only stairs.

It was terrifying. The vast spaces on all sides of him, the precariousness of his position were enough to make his sight dim and the blood rush from his head. And the stairs, twisting around him in senseless complexity, end-less, going nowhere, dizzied him, sending him stumbling backwards against—

He spun around, stopping himself just in time from plunging into the gleaming white void behind him. There was nothing there but empty space, and more stairs. But the elevator—there had to be a wall for the elevator to move in! But there was nothing. It must have been some sort of electronic bucket on a chain. Shaking, he sank to his knees at the base of a flight of steps leading up from the landing. He wrapped his arms around himself and dropped his head onto his chest, closing his eyes, and tried his best not to move, or to think.

Why had they put him here? It must be some kind of

punishment, but what had he done wrong? They *had* been strange to him recently, he began to realize, going over the past week in his mind. The lingering looks he had noticed, as though he were ill; little extra gestures of concern, like the second piece of pie he had been given at lunch yesterday. While they had been happening he hadn't seen any significance to them, but now, putting them all together, a pattern began to emerge. But it was not a pattern that should have led to punishment; it was more as though they knew he was about to undergo a dangerous operation.

But it didn't make sense. This wasn't a hospital, and it *was* punishment. It was horrible here. Even though his eyes were tightly shut he could not lose the feeling of where he was. The smallness and the vulnerability of his perch made his skin prickle and his head begin to spin again. *No!* he tried to tell himself, *Think about something else, think about being in bed, under the covers.* But before he could do that the other thought came, even more terrifying: *How long am I going to be here?* Involuntarily he moaned. *Maybe it isn't just going to be for a few minutes or hours; maybe I'll be here for days; maybe forever.*

He couldn't bear it. Even an hour in this place would drive him mad. But maybe . . . maybe there was a way out, maybe he could escape.

Slowly he opened his eyes. Very carefully he moved his head around, without getting up, and looked up the steps behind him. If he was going to find a way out, he might as well start there. But they were so narrow, vanishing up into whiteness, so steep, so high, and there were no railings. No, he couldn't go up them; he couldn't go down either. What if he should get dizzy again, and slip,

5

or take the wrong step? No, it was safer to stay here, and wait. Perhaps something would happen; perhaps they had made a mistake, and someone would come and get him out. He closed his eyes again, pressing himself against the stairs.

chapter 2

Walking down the corridor at the old orphanage, the first orphanage, the one he loved. His room. His and Jasper's room. The window seat, the two beds. Jasper looking up from his desk, smiling, glad to see him. Jasper saying something. Something very important. The most important message, the secret message. But the buses, the buses were so loud, he couldn't hear him. "Louder, Jasper, louder!" But Jasper keeps smiling, keeps talking, doesn't notice. Millions of voices, and the matron and the doctor are there, and the wardens and the social workers, and the foster parents, and Jasper is off in the corner, he can't see him anymore, can't hear him. What was the message, Jasper? What was the message?

A shiver went through him. He swayed, lifting his sweaty forehead from his arms. It took him a moment to realize where he was, and that he must have been dreaming. The dream had been beautiful at the beginning, terrible at the end, but he longed to be in it again. If only he hadn't awakened!

That was when he noticed the figure moving far below him. A very small figure with dark hair, walking up a flight of steps. His heart began to beat furiously. He started to call out, but at the first croaking sound his voice caught in his throat, and he blushed. Very slowly and cautiously, resting his hand on a step, he stood up. He began to be conscious of the regular sound of footsteps in the vast quietness, as the person below marched up the stairs. Obviously it was someone familiar with this place, for there was no hesitation in his gait, no apprehension as he looked calmly from side to side. It must be someone coming to get him out. *I have to call out to him,* Peter said to himself. *What if he doesn't find me, and goes away, and just leaves me here?*

This thought was enough to bring out his voice. "Hey?" he said falteringly, and then more loudly, "Hey!" Still not a shout, but enough to make the figure below stop and look around. "Up here!" Peter stammered. "Above you!"

The black head below him suddenly became white as the person looked up at him. The hair was quite short, but the pointed face was thin and delicate, and Peter could not tell if it was a boy or a girl. The voice, however, though rather rough, was distinctly feminine. "Hey!" she shouted up at him, her words carrying clearly across the space between them. "What *is* this?"

"Wh-what?" Peter murmured, more to himself than to her. But that must mean she didn't know any more than he did! The disappointment made him feel faint. "But don't you know?" he said.

"Speak up!" she shouted, her hand at her ear. "Can't hear you!"

"But don't you even *know*?" he screamed, clenching

8

his fists, his throat suddenly clogged with tears. "Don't you *know*?"

"No, I do *not* know!" she shouted back, her hands on her hips, "but I'm gonna find out pretty quick." And she began running up the stairs.

As she bounded toward him, he reflected that even if she couldn't get him out, it was probably better to have her here than to be alone. Although she *was* a bit frightening; he wished it could have been someone who seemed gentler. He looked aside as she reached his landing, too shy to meet her gaze.

She was a little shorter than he, and had to stand quite close, the landing was so small. He turned to look at her. But the black eyes in her olive-skinned face were so direct and penetrating, yet speculative, that he quickly looked away again.

"So you don't know where the hell we are either?" she said.

Peter shook his head, a little startled by her use of profanity. "No . . . um, somebody . . . they just took me here, they blindfolded me and just left me here. I don't know anything."

"Me either. And they pulled that blindfold stunt on me, too. I knew they had it in for me, but I never thought they'd do anything like *this*. Who brought you here, anyway? I mean, you must have known who it was, if they took you away from home and all."

"But they didn't. I mean . . . I don't have a home. I don't have any parents. I live in an orphanage."

"So do I."

"You do?"

She nodded.

"So today they just called me to the office," he continued, looking down at his feet, "and blindfolded me, and told me to go with the person who was there. And they tied my hands—"

"Can't you talk any louder? I'm right next to you and I can hardly hear a thing you're saying."

He raised his voice with an effort. "And took me in this car, and brought me here, and took the blindfold off, and that's all."

"Yeah, same with me. Except I thought I knew what they were doing. They'd been threatening to throw me in reform school for months, and after that last little trick I pulled—" She paused and chuckled to herself, "—after *that*, I thought, sure thing, they finally did it. But you—hey, look at me, I don't bite—"

He raised his head, his eyes wavering across her face.

"You don't exactly seem the type who'd do anything, ah, anything they'd get after you for."

"No," he said, "I never did anything they didn't like. That's why I can't understand why . . . why they *did* this to me."

"Yeah. Well I don't get it either, because if you're here it couldn't be like a punishment thing. So you're an orphan, too. That's kind of interesting. It must mean *something*. . . ."

"Mmm," he said. It was awkward, standing so close to her, so carefully he stepped back and sat down on the second step, looking over both sides to make sure he was exactly in the middle.

"But the question is, how do we get out?" she went on. "Got any ideas?"

He shook his head.

"Yeah. Well, let's see. . . ." She was wearing jeans and a tight black T-shirt, standing with her feet apart and her arms folded across her thin chest. She took a package of cigarettes out of her pants pocket and held it out to him; he shook his head. Smoking was a serious offense, but she seemed perfectly comfortable as she pulled out a cigarette with her lips, lit the match with one hand and brought it to the tip of the cigarette, then flicked the match down into the void.

"Let's see," she continued, blowing out smoke. "The thing I can't figure out is, are we aboveground, underground, or what. I mean, if we knew we were aboveground, the way out would be down there; if we knew we were *under*ground, the way out would be up. Could you tell, when they brought you here?"

"No."

"Neither could I. That must have been part of it, the rats; not to let us know where we are."

"What—" He hesitated, then went on. "What was the . . . the trick you said you did?"

"Huh? Oh, *that*!" She smiled. It was a conspiratorial smile; and her eyes, wrinkling at the corners, lost some of their wariness. "See, there's this big cow of a matron at the house I live in, and she really hates my guts. God, all the extra stuff I always have to do! And lectures, 'Young ladies don't do this, young ladies don't do that,' it all made me want to puke. So the other day . . ." She giggled, "I snuck into the science room (you can get past the electric eyes if you crawl, you know), and there's this snake there, in a cage. Just a black snake, scared to death of people. So I broke open the cage and took the snake—"

"You picked it up?"

11

"Sure. Why not? And I took it down the hall—I had to hide it under my shirt so they wouldn't see it on the video screens—and got into the matron's room. That was kind of tricky, I had to get in through the window by climbing out along this ledge with that snake squirming all over me. And then I put it in her bed, and got the hell out of there. Not that it made any difference; she knew it was me, of course."

"But what happened?"

"Well, I sort of wanted to hang around that end of the building, but of course there's bed check, and anyway, it would have been kind of suspicious. It didn't matter in the end, the way she yelled, the whole dormitory heard it. Everybody sat up in bed, saying, 'What's that? What's that?'" She mimicked mousy feminine voices. "But I kept my mouth shut, not wanting to give myself away." She took a deep drag on her cigarette and dropped it casually over the edge. "They dragged me into her office the next morning, and she didn't even bawl me out, she was just real quiet and tense, it was kind of scary. But worth it, to hear the old cow scream like that. . . . Anyway, that was two days ago, and now they blindfold me and bring me here. I thought it was because of that, but now, I don't know."

"Mmmm," Peter said.

"You sure don't talk much. What's your name? Mine's Lola."

"Peter."

"How old are you? I'm sixteen."

"So am I."

"Hmmm, that's also kind of interesting. Both from state 'homes'"—she said the word with an ironic twist—"and both sixteen."

"I don't care if it's interesting or not," he forced himself to say. "I just want to get out of here. I *hate* it!"

"Well, if you hate it so much, kiddo, why don't you do something about it?"

"Oh, I don't know. . . ." His voice trailed off again from its brief emotional burst, returning to the barely audible murmur in which he habitually spoke. "What is there to do? Just . . ." He sighed, "just wait until they come to get us out."

"But who says they're *gonna* come and get us out, huh? *I'm* not gonna wait around in this . . . this . . ." She gestured, "this . . . *place* till some administrator out there remembers we're here. I'm gonna find the way out. And if you don't want to stay here till you starve to death, I'd advise you to come with me. I don't know what they're trying to do, but I don't trust them, not one little bit. Come on!"

"But. . . ." He remembered how confidently she had negotiated the steps, and his own fears. But she was probably right; his only hope was to go with her. He got to his feet, rather unsteadily, not looking down.

"Now, up or down? Don't you have any ideas?" She paused only briefly. "All right, I'll say . . . down. This place is just too big to be underground." And she started down the steps at a quick pace.

He began following her very slowly. It was horrible; every time he took a step he pictured himself plunging forward into empty space. He went carefully, setting both feet firmly on each step before descending to the next. Very soon she was far below him.

She stopped to wait for him at another small landing. "Can't you go any faster?" she said when he approached. "We'll never get anywhere at this rate."

"But I . . ." he began. It was useless; she, who was so unafraid, would never understand. The hopelessness of the situation rose up inside him in a wave of self-pity. He swallowed, unable to keep his eyes from filling with tears.

She was watching his face. "Oh, well," she said, her voice suddenly softer. "Big deal. It probably doesn't make any difference anyway. Go as slow as you want. I'll stay with you."

She kept just ahead of him as they went on, turning back often to talk. "So what's your life story? What about your parents? Did you ever know them?"

"No. I . . . can't remember anything about them. They told me that my father . . . died in the war—"

"Same as everybody else."

"—and my mother . . . she died in a car crash."

"What kinda place they put you in?"

"Oh . . . different ones."

"Yeah? What were they like?"

He thought of the first place, the one they had moved him from just three years ago. It had been an old building, with windows that opened and every room a different shape, with beds and desks that weren't part of the wall and they let you move around the way you wanted. The one where the matron had especially liked him, and the teachers had been interesting and kind. The one where he and Jasper had been roommates, and best friends. Jasper, who had always taken care of him. He would probably never see Jasper again. . . .

"Well?"

"Oh." He had forgotten where he was, losing himself in memories; but somehow he had managed to keep walking. "I was in one place . . . for a long time. It was . . .

it was real good there." She looked back, noticing the new sound in his voice, then turned quickly away. "But then, they moved me, three years ago, to another place—"

"The rats!" she interrupted quietly, but with surprising vehemence.

"—that was real big, and . . . I didn't know anybody. Then they kept moving me to different ones, because I kept . . . not adjusting. And then, today I thought, I thought they were just taking me to another one."

"Yeah," she said, and stopped walking. They had reached another landing, where the stairway divided into three parts: two flights going up, and a narrow bridge without railings fifteen feet long, connecting to another flight. There was still no bottom in sight, just more stairs crisscrossing below them.

"We're not getting anywhere," Lola said, looking down. "Except it seems like there's more stairs down there, closer together." She turned to him. "Listen, we're gonna have to cross that bridge. I know you don't want to, but it's the only way to keep going down. I'll go first."

The bridge was only about a foot wide, arching slightly. Even Lola seemed rather hesitant as she stepped onto it, and it took Peter nearly ten minutes to inch his way across. Down they continued, until suddenly Lola stopped short and he almost bumped into her. "Wait a minute," she said slowly. "Something weird here. . . . It's getting harder and harder to go down. I mean, there's all those stairs down there but. . . ." From the landing below them, three flights went up, none went down. "But it's like they don't want us to get to them." She looked behind her. "Sorry, kid, but we're gonna have to go back and take that bridge up there. This way goes nowhere."

Backtracking became more frequent, for it was difficult to see very far ahead, and any direction that looked promising seemed eventually to direct them upward again. Nevertheless there were always stairs below them to hide whatever bottom there might be. Their progress became more horizontal than vertical, with more bridges to negotiate, and these continued to be a trial for Peter. At last Lola noticed his shaken condition. "Hey, wanna sit down?" she said, as they stepped off a bridge onto a landing hardly big enough for them both.

"Oh, yes," he said gratefully, and immediately sat down on a step. Lola reclined across from him, stretching out her legs and resting her feet on either side of his. She lit another cigarette, then put her hands behind her head as she puffed, the cigarette dangling from her thin lips.

"Now I'm beginning to figure this place out," she said. "Maybe there *is* a way out down there, or up there," she jerked her head in that direction. "But they don't want us to get to it. These cruddy stairs just don't connect. There's no way to get to those stairs down there."

"Mmm," he said. Inside himself he knew that the situation was, of course, hopeless; and that it was only a matter of time until even she would have to give up. But in the meantime it was diverting to follow along after her; there was, after all, nothing else to do, except dream.

chapter 3

Lola watched the pale, fleshy face in its frame of whitish blond hair slowly grow glazed, the eyes staring off unfocused into the distance. She had already typed him as one of those shy, sensitive creeps. The kind who never wanted to have any fun because he was always afraid of getting caught. Why didn't he realize that the whole point was to get away with things, to prove that you were better than all those stupid administrators, with all their stupid rules?

So now they had put her in here. She glanced around again. In a way she was almost glad. It was better than being in solitary or cleaning the toilets. It was more interesting, for one thing, and kind of a challenge. The question was, why had they put *him* here? He had obviously never dared to break a rule in his life. Sometime she would have to figure that one out.

In the meantime she was getting hungry. Now that she had decided, for the time being, to stop looking for the way out, food was beginning to be her main concern. Food had always come regularly before, but now that the situation she was in was completely different and unknown, it was possible that the food situation might be different too. Assuming they were going to be here for any length of time, it somehow didn't seem possible that someone would come and bring it to them—that just wouldn't fit in with this place. What if there wasn't going to be any food, then what would she do?

She tossed her cigarette away and looked at Peter. "Hey!" she said. He started, and his eyes came back to her face. "You hungry?" she asked.

"Um . . . no, I . . . I wasn't thinking about it."

The mumbling, hesitant quality of his speech irritated her. She did feel sorry for the poor kid; he'd probably had it rough; but it would have been better to be here with somebody who could help. She was going to have to take care of him as well as herself. "Well, *I'm* hungry," she said, and stood up. "Come on, come on, honey, you've had your rest. Time to get moving again."

Now she proceeded in an upward direction, but also moving across, changing stairways frequently. She knew it was rather aimless; but she also knew that the only thing to do was to explore, to see as much as possible, in the faint hope that something might be different somewhere. But even in a million years would she ever get to know this place? It was impossible to tell whether or not they had been in a particular spot before, whether they were covering new ground or just going in circles. And it didn't help to have to go so slow! Why couldn't he get used to it?

She fought down a growing feeling of desperation. She

couldn't give up, she *had* to keep believing that there might be a way out, that something might change. If there was anything at all to be done, she was determined to discover it; and since feeling desperate would only make it more difficult, she refused to allow herself that luxury.

Being ravenously hungry, of course, did not help. She had only missed one, perhaps two meals, and already it was growing more and more difficult to ignore the empty feeling in her stomach. How would she feel after another day or two? She had always tried to be tough, and was determined not to weaken now, but she had never really been faced with hunger before, and was not sure how to handle it. She even began to imagine that she was smelling food, and cursed herself for being so vulnerable.

And then she stopped, motioning behind her with her hand for Peter to keep quiet. She waited, hardly breathing, and the sound came again. It was an undefinable series of noises, partly whirring and mechanical, but also strangely moist. Slurping, she would have called it. "Did you hear that?" she asked, turning to Peter.

"I guess . . . ," he said vaguely.

"Well, *listen!* I want to know what you think it is. You've got to do *some*thing to help, every once in a while!"

His eyes grew moist.

"And don't start crying. I'm being nicer than you deserve. Just listen!"

"Yes . . . I hear it, for sure," he said at last. "It sounds like . . . like some kind of machine that makes animal noises."

"Yeah. It sounds kinda like that to me too." She was

indecisive only for a moment. Though there was certainly something menacing about the sound, any change would be better than this endless and aimless climbing. "Let's see, it sounds like it's over there. . . ."

At first it was difficult to tell exactly which way to go, but after a few wrong guesses the sound began to grow steadily nearer. Soon it was quite clear that it was coming from a landing directly above them. The sound was quite regular: a whirring, a few soft clicks, then wet, chewing noises, a little pause, and the whirring would begin the pattern again. And the smell of food—of good food—was stronger now. Perhaps it wasn't just her imagination.

The spiral stairway they were climbing led to a round hole in the landing, near the edge, through which they would have to climb to reach the top. Lola paused for a moment, her head just below the hole, then took three quick steps and poked her head through.

One inch from her nose was a bulge of white cloth, and it took her a moment to realize that it was a person, sitting on the floor with her back to the hole. A very fat person, with an abundance of golden curls tumbling down over her round back to the bulges at her waist. Still silently, Lola crept up a few more steps until she could peer over the girl's shoulder. In front of the girl, built into the floor, was a plastic hemisphere about a foot in diameter, made up of many diamond-shaped facets. It was red, and had a faint glow. As Lola watched, the girl leaned forward, peered into the plastic, and stuck out her tongue. Immediately the whirring began, then the clicks, and a brown cylinder rolled out of the slot. The girl was ready for it, her hand poised, and it had hardly appeared before it was in her mouth. Then came the animal sounds.

Stifling a gasp, Lola watched in amazement. Without pausing, the girl leaned forward the instant she had swallowed the food and stuck out her tongue again. There was the whirring, the clicking, the brown cylinder rolling into her hand, and then the noisy eating.

The next time, Lola was ready. Moving quickly, she leaped to the landing and grabbed the cylinder the instant it appeared.

The girl shrieked, and Peter's head bobbed down out of sight through the hole. Her hand over her mouth, the girl stared at Lola. Her features seemed small, lost in mounds of pink flesh; and her body jiggled underneath the white ruffles of her dress as she pressed herself backwards against a flight of steps. Lola was poised on the lower steps of another flight, across from the girl, her arms folded across her chest and the cylinder swinging casually from one hand.

"Oh, my," the girl said, taking her hand from her mouth and pressing it against her. "Oh, my, you scared me!"

"Well what else could I do, seeing you eating up all that food and me starving to death, huh?" Lola smiled thinly at her, her head to one side.

"Yes, but—" said the girl, and then uttered another little squeal as Peter poked up his head once again.

"Come on up, Pete," Lola said. "There isn't much room up here, but there's food."

The landing was a sort of crossroads, four flights of steps rising up from it, each opposite another, as well as the spiral stairway from below. The hole and the food apparatus and the fat girl took up all the floor space, so Peter sat down hesitantly on one of the stairways.

If she had to pick the two worst people in the world to

be here with, Lola reflected with irony, it would certainly be these creeps. She studied the cylinder in her hand. It was different from the synthetic protein she was used to, and had a tantalizing smell. She bit off the end and began to chew. An incredibly rich, succulent flavor filled her mouth. She took another bite, and another, suddenly understanding the fat girl's piggishness. It was the most delicious thing she had ever tasted.

"My God!" she said, swallowing the last bit. "What *is* this? It's fantastic!"

"Meat," said the girl. Her voice was high-pitched and babyish. "It's real meat. I can tell." She was staring at Lola; there was an unexpected hardness in her small eyes. They were like a doll's eyes, strangely emotionless; and, to her surprise, Lola felt a pang of fear. But in a moment the girl looked down and edged toward the red structure on the floor.

"Hey," said Lola, as the girl moved the next cylinder toward her mouth. The girl stopped, her mouth open, her eyes on Lola. "Give it to him," Lola said slowly, making her voice as tough as possible; something about the girl's eyes had put her on the defensive. "It might be the last one."

The girl looked around to where Peter was sitting, and with obvious reluctance stretched her pudgy arm toward him. He took the meat and nibbled at it cautiously.

"And the next one's mine," Lola went on, nearly snarling. "You've had plenty."

"Then get it yourself!" said the girl. She moved her rear end up onto a step. "I think you're mean."

Feeling foolish, Lola kneeled on the landing and bent over the screen. She stuck out her tongue. Nothing happened.

"Hey!" she said, and stuck it out again, farther, leaning closer to the glass. But again, nothing happened.

"Ha ha," said the girl, not laughing. "It doesn't work when *you* do it."

Nor did it work when Lola made Peter do it, or when she tried again. At last, returning to her steps, Lola said, "Okay, you try again."

And it worked. "Here," said the girl, handing Peter the first piece. "You can have as much as you want. But *she* isn't getting any. She's too mean."

"Aw, cut it out," said Lola, trying to sound casual but actually feeling rather worried. "Look, I was just trying to make sure we got some too. I mean, who knows how much is in there? It could have run out any time."

"But you didn't have to be so mean about it," said the girl, staring at Lola as she chewed. "And you didn't have to scare me at first. You almost made me throw *up*. And I could have fallen off. You should be careful in a place like this, so high up and— Oh! What is this place anyway? When are they going to come and get us out?"

"We don't know any more than you do. They may never come and get us out. Which is why we gotta try to get along, and *share* things." It was almost more than Lola could bear, being so hungry, and at the mercy of this creature.

"You don't know where we are either? Either of you?" said the girl. "But . . . but I don't under*stand*." She swallowed, then leaned forward and stuck out her little red tongue automatically, reaching out her hand to catch the food without even looking at it. "I mean," she went on, chewing, and pointedly ignoring Lola's hungry eyes, "why did they bring me here? I didn't do anything wrong. And all these steps, what are they for?"

23

"Wish I could answer that one for you," said Lola. "And, ah, by the way, next time you get a chance, toss one of those sticks over this way."

"Oh, all right," said the girl, and handed her the next one.

Lola ate quickly. "How'd you figure out how to do that, anyway?" she said when she finished, lighting a cigarette.

"You *smoke*?" the girl said, amazed. "But I thought only—" Suddenly she stopped.

"Sure I smoke. I'm not gonna let anybody tell me what not to do. And you thought only what?"

"Oh, nothing, nothing," the girl said quickly. "I didn't mean anything."

"Mmm," said Lola, watching her, wondering what she was trying to cover up. "Well anyway, did they put you down right here, or what?"

"No. See, I was blindfolded, and they let me off somewhere up there," she gestured vaguely. "So then, I didn't understand, and I was afraid, and I didn't know what to do, so I just waited there for awhile, but nothing happened. And then I thought, well, maybe there's a way out, so I started walking down the steps."

This babe is not nearly as helpless as she at first appears, thought Lola.

"Then I got to this landing, and I saw this screen and thought maybe it was a way of communicating. So I kept talking into it, and then yelling and screaming into it, but nothing happened, so I got mad and stuck out my tongue. And then the meat came out. At first I couldn't figure out why, or what made it happen, and I tried *everything*, and it didn't work, and then I stuck my tongue out again, and more meat came out, and then I knew."

"How come you're so sure it's real meat?"

"I . . ." Suddenly the girl seemed confused. "I . . . I just know, that's all. I . . . My mother and father." She sighed. "They . . . they had it once."

"Your mother and father? You mean you have parents?"

"So what if I do? What's wrong with that?"

"Nothing at all. It's just that both of us are from state homes, and I sorta figured anybody else in this place would be too."

"Well, as a matter of fact, I don't have parents." She looked down for a moment. "My mother and father . . . about a month ago, they died in a car crash. And since then, I've been in a weird place, this real high-security place, and they kept giving me these . . . these tests. It was *horrible*. Then today they brought me here." Still kneeling on the landing, she leaned forward and stuck out her tongue. But this time there was no whir or click, and no more food.

Lola could not help but smile to herself at the girl's attempts to get the machine to respond, having been in the same position herself just a little while before. The girl blew and puffed, dribbling little bits of saliva down onto the screen.

"You might as well give up," Lola said at last, tossing away her cigarette. "The machine thinks you've had enough. And it's right."

"Oh, shut up!" said the girl, who seemed close to tears. "Ever since you came along you've been saying mean things, and bossing me around, and acting like I'm pitiful, and—"

"Who said—?"

"It isn't just what you said, it was the way you acted.

Because I'm fat, you think I'm not as good as you. But you'll see, you'll see who wins in the end. I *hate* you!"

"What the hell are you talking about, winning and stuff?" said Lola, stunned. "You act like we're having a war or something."

"We are. And you started it."

"Oh, come off it. It's stupid to fight. What I wanna know is, what made the machine work in the first place? Why in *hell* sticking out your tongue should make it work. . . . It doesn't make any sense, no sense at all, like everything else here." She looked in frustration from one face to the other. Peter's was glazing over again, and the girl was staring petulantly off into the distance. Once more she cursed her luck for being in here with them; and she cursed it too for being in here at all. Yes, it was a game, a challenge, and she wanted to win. But it was a game with no apparent logic or rules. For the second time, but not for the last, black fingers of doubt crept into her usually confident mind.

"Hello," said a voice from above, a gentle, musical voice. "I'm so glad I found you at last."

chapter 4

Peter was startled. No one had said anything for quite a while, and then suddenly there was this new voice. He looked up.

A girl was standing on the stairway across from him. She was slender and tall. Her face, with its small chin and rather prominent nose, was not exactly pretty; but her serene expression, and the pale, shining hair falling to her waist, made her beautiful. "I . . . heard your voices," she said, looking back and forth between them, a tentative smile hovering around her thin lips. "And I've been looking for you for awhile. I was so glad. For a long time I thought I was . . . all alone here."

"Uh . . . glad to see you," Lola said. "Come on down."

"Okay," said the girl, sitting down on a step and tossing her hair back with her hand. Her gray institutional dress, which would have looked dreary on most people, was somehow flattering on her. "I'm kind of disappointed, actually. When I first heard voices I thought it meant I

27

would be able to get out, or at least find out what was happening. But then I heard what you were just saying, about nothing making sense here, and I guess . . . well, you probably don't know any more than me."

"Right," Lola said.

"But what were you saying about . . ." Her face twisted into a rather humorous, quizzical expression, "about sticking out your tongue, and making it work?"

"The food thing," the fat girl said, pointing at the floor. "See? I found it first," and she shot Lola a chilling glance, "and I figured out that if you stuck your tongue out at that screen, food would come out. Good food. But then *she* came along—and him too—and she kept being mean, and then it stopped working."

"But how strange that it should work that way," said the new girl, smiling around at the three of them. "Why . . .?"

Lola shrugged her shoulders. "Who knows? You hungry? Maybe it'll work again."

"No, no thanks. Not now." There was a silence as the three of them stared at the newcomer. She shifted uncomfortably. "Well, um, what are your names? Mine's Abigail."

"Lola," said Lola. "And this is Peter. And you?" She looked at the fat girl.

"Blossom," the fat girl said, rather reluctantly but with a haughty toss of her head, and Lola snorted. "Blossom Pilkington," she went on. "And you can just shut up! I *knew* you'd do that."

Lola turned to Abigail. "You an orphan?" she asked.

Abigail nodded. "I never knew my parents. I've always lived in state homes. But how did you know?"

"Me and Peter are just the same."

"I knew my parents," Blossom said. "They died about a month ago. And before they died we lived in a real—" Suddenly she stopped, and then sighed.

Lola studied Blossom for a moment, then said, "And me and Peter are sixteen."

"So am I," said the others together.

"Well, so now we know everything," Lola said, standing up and stretching. "But I wonder how many *more* sixteen-year-old orphans are gonna show up? If any."

"It does seem sort of strange, that there's a boy here," Abigail said, looking at Peter. "You'd think they wouldn't put us in here together."

"Why?" said Lola. "After all, nothing in this place makes sense." She put her hands on her hips. "But I'm getting tired of just sitting here. I wonder if there's any other things like this?" She touched the screen with her foot. "And there's a couple of other things I'm beginning to wonder: Is there any water around, for instance; and is there a toilet?"

"That's right," said Abigail.

"Yeah," said Lola. "You can have all the food you want, but you can't live if there's no water. And we *are* gonna have to go to the bathroom sometime. We could always just do it off the edge—" (Blossom pursed her lips and looked down at her lap.) "—but that might get kinda messy after a while. And I bet there is a toilet somewhere, if we can only find it. This place is all so sparkling clean and pure; whatever it's for, going on the floor isn't part of it. I'm gonna look around. Anybody coming? . . . No? . . . Okay." She turned and ran lightly up the stairs.

"Whew! Am I glad *she's* gone," Blossom said, the moment Lola was out of earshot.

"Why?" said Abigail. "What's wrong with her?"

"I guess you didn't notice. For some reason she was trying to be nice to you, but she was horrible to me. Wasn't she?" she turned on Peter.

"Um . . . I don't know."

"But you heard the things she said," Blossom insisted. "They *were* mean, you've got to admit it."

What could he say? She was right in a sense, and he longed to agree with her, just to get her to leave him alone. But he did feel a vague loyalty to Lola, a reluctance to speak against her.

Finally, however, with both of them staring at him, he gave in. "Yes, she was mean, I guess."

Did Blossom really smile slightly, or was it only a little twitch in her puffy cheek as she turned back to Abigail? "See?" she said. "He thought she was too."

Abigail seemed rather embarrassed. "Oh, all right. But you can hardly blame anybody for acting funny in this place. It's so scary, not knowing why we're here, or what's going to happen to us."

"But you . . . you don't seem frightened," Peter said. "Even . . . even when you first found us, you were so . . . calm about it."

"Was I?" Her pale cheeks flushed slightly. "Well, I *am* frightened, but I guess I don't . . . I'm just the way I am."

"Well, I'm not *that* frightened," said Blossom. "I mean, somebody's going to come and get us out pretty soon, of course. This is all just a big mistake. It has to be."

Abigail's eyes met Peter's for a moment. There was really nothing to say, Blossom was so positive. Peter wanted to believe her, it would be so nice if he could. But he knew they didn't make mistakes like this.

"You've been in state homes all your life?" Abigail asked him, breaking the silence that followed Blossom's outburst.

He nodded. "And you?" he asked, trying to turn the conversation away from himself. "What . . . what kind of place were you in?"

"Oh, it was okay. I guess I've been lucky. It wasn't one of those huge ones. It was kind of small, and the teachers were nice, and I have some good friends."

"You mean you don't hate it?" Blossom sounded incredulous.

"No."

"But there must have been some teachers that were horrible, and some creepy kids that you hated."

"Well, yes, there were, I guess."

"Well, you don't have to sound so snooty about it," said Blossom. "What's wrong with hating somebody? *'Loathing is endless,'*" she quoted in her high-pitched, nasal voice. "*'Hate is a bottomless cup. I pour and pour.'* Did you ever hear that? It's from some ancient play or something."

"No." Abigail seemed embarrassed again.

"That was the only good thing about being in the place I've been since my parents died." She spoke of their death easily now, as though they had gone for a holiday at a resort development. "There were so many people to hate, that's what was good about it. But I had *friends* too, good friends, at the school I went to before my parents died." She paused. "Do you . . . do you want to know something? Something about my parents?" She looked eagerly back and forth between then, and her voice dropped to a whisper. "I probably shouldn't tell you, I know I'm not supposed to talk about it, but . . . well, since they did put

31

me in here with you, and everything is so strange, maybe it's okay." She folded her arms. "Anyway, I *want* to tell. I bet you won't believe it. But it's true, it's really true."

Suddenly Peter wanted to know what she was going to say. There was something strangely compelling about the eagerness in her voice; and Abigail, who had been staring into her lap, was now watching Blossom just as intently as he.

"Listen," Blossom said. "Listen." She spoke very slowly and distinctly. "We lived in a *house*. With real grass around it, and a live growing tree." She sat up a little straighter, watching for their reaction.

"A house?" Abigail said. "But—"

"Yes." Blossom nodded. "Some people still live in their own private houses. You didn't know that, did you? Hardly anybody knows. I mean, the *President* lives in one, everybody knows that. But some of his top advisers do too, his chief aides and advisers. There's a whole neighborhood with houses in it, and a big wall around it. Of course it's a secret, because if anyone outside knew about the houses, they would think it wasn't fair, and it would be bad for the administration's image. So we went to a special school; they never let us meet outsiders. And our house had a swimming pool, and a special room to eat in, that wasn't the kitchen, a room just for eating. And sometimes my mother even made our own food, and it was so good. Oh, it was so good." She clasped her hands together, and for a moment her eyes slipped shut and her head tilted back in a kind of reverie.

Peter found that he was listening closely to her, hanging on every word, just as Abigail was doing. He couldn't deny that Blossom could be fascinating, almost charming

in some odd way. And even though her story was prepos-
terous, she spoke with such intensity and conviction that
it was difficult not to believe her.

"Really?" said Abigail skeptically.

"Yes," Blossom insisted. "My father was a psychiatrist.
He checked people out, people they were thinking of hir-
ing. And that's why we got to live in a house, and have
meat every week, and a pool, even though all the press
releases said we lived in residential megastructures like
everybody else."

Peter leaned back again. Blossom's story was a direct
contradiction of information that had been drummed into
him for his whole life, but nevertheless he believed her.
Why should I make it up? her tone implied with every
matter-of-fact word. It was the same way when she had
gotten him to admit that Lola was mean; Lola really had
been mean, after all.

"I just thought of something," Blossom said. "The food
thing doesn't work for me anymore, and it *never* worked
for them, but maybe it would work for you. Why don't
you try it, Abigail?"

"I'm not really hungry," Abigail said.

"Me either," said Blossom. "But I mean, what else is
there to do until they come to get us out? Come on, just
try it? Just get down there and stick out your tongue."

"Well . . ." said Abigail. She was clearly uncomfortable.
Peter wished Blossom would leave her alone.

"But why not?" Blossom said. "Are you afraid?"

Abigail shook her head. "No. It's just that . . . I'm not
hungry now. And if you're the only one it ever worked for,
then you should probably try."

"Well, all right," said Blossom. "I'll do it now. But I'll

get you to do it *some*time." And once again she began laboring awkwardly over the screen.

Peter closed his eyes. It was difficult at first to get into the daydream; the hard realities on the other side of his eyelids did not want to retreat. But gradually his head began to fill with warmth. The steps dissolved into a white mist, and back through the mist came his old room, his and Jasper's room. *Jasper, sitting on the bed and taking off his shoes, smiling, punching Peter on the shoulder and telling him not to worry. "You're okay, Pete, you're better than a hundred of those slobs put together. Tomorrow I'll tell them so myself." Jasper's strong, hard body as he got into bed, so different from Peter's. Strong, to protect him, to take care of him. Jasper, who always took care of him—*

"What?" said a voice. It sounded real, but it was a familiar voice, and Peter knew it was part of his daydream. How strange, that the dream should sound so real. "What," said the voice again, "are you doing down on the floor like that?" And there were footsteps, and he heard Blossom's noises stop. But that voice, how could it be real? Apprehensively, he opened his eyes.

His feet on the spiral stairs, the top half of his body already through the hole, looking around at the three of them with an expression of amused bewilderment on his face, stood Jasper.

chapter 5

Abigail hadn't heard the boy approach either. She had been sitting there trying not to look at Blossom and making an effort not to get weepy about being here, when suddenly someone said something and there was a boy, a very attractive boy, climbing quickly up to the landing.

"What," he said, looking around at them briskly, "are you doing down on the floor like that?" Blossom was perusing him from her kneeling position, and Peter was gaping at him, his usually expressionless face spread wide open in disbelief. Abigail couldn't imagine why he should seem so surprised; it had been startling to see the boy appear, but it wasn't as if he were a ghost or anything.

"Food," Blossom said, pulling herself up to her step and still eyeing the boy. "Food used to come out of that slot. I was trying to make it come out again." As she explained, the boy turned away from her to look appraisingly at Abigail. His eyes were a very intense shade of blue-gray. Abigail met his gaze for a moment, then looked down, a flutter of excitement beginning in her stomach. Already his arrival had changed the situation completely for her. Blossom and Lola, after all, were girls. And Peter, though he seemed nice, wasn't very good-looking and was so terribly shy. But this new boy! He was just the kind of boy who got her all stirred up, who distracted her, who made it practically impossible to think about anything else. And even though she knew that it was wrong to have such feelings, she could not make them go away.

She looked up at him again. He already seemed slightly bored by Blossom's explanation of the food machine, staring off into the distance and tapping his foot restlessly. His dark blond hair was just curly enough, Abigail reflected, and just the right length to set off the planes of his lean face. He was wearing athletic clothes—a white T-shirt and gray sweat pants—but they certainly looked good on him: It was clear that the body underneath, which he held erectly, was hard and smooth-muscled.

And of course it wasn't just the way he looked, it was the confidence and energy and potential high spirits that he exuded. They rippled in the air around him like waves from a pebble tossed into a pond. Though his presence made her tense, Abigail nevertheless felt suddenly more comfortable, more at home, than she had felt since she had entered this place.

Peter was still gaping at him, but now he seemed puzzled. "And now it doesn't work at all, nobody can make it work," Blossom finished, and, with a quick glance in Abigail's direction, the boy turned to Peter, really looking at him for the first time. Abigail felt her heart contract in a sudden spasm of pity—the expression on Peter's face had become so unutterably pleading and pathetic, like a begging dog looking up at his master. But why?

The new boy didn't seem to notice. "So," he said, "you the only other guy? Anybody else around?"

Peter was studying his face intensely. And all at once his expression faded, the life in it suddenly draining away. He looked down.

"Huh?" said the boy.

"Um . . . there's another girl," Peter said, his voice fuzzy. "Lola. We haven't found anyone else yet."

"So it's us two guys alone with three girls, huh?" Grinning, the boy cuffed him lightly on the shoulder and Peter flinched. Then he sighed and looked up again.

"What . . . what's your name?" Peter said.

"Oliver." He turned and stepped lightly over to the empty flight, sat down, resting his elbows on a step behind, and looked around at them again. "Two guys and three girls," he went on. "So far. And nobody knows a thing. Including me. There I am, just leaving the locker room to go to soccer practice, and they call my name over the loud-speaker to come to the office, and then they blindfold me, and bring me to this . . . *this* crazy place."

"The same thing happened to all of us," said Blossom. "And we're all orphans, and all sixteen."

"Really? No kidding! Me too." He chuckled briefly, shaking his head. It bothered Abigail a little. He was taking the whole thing too lightly; somehow it didn't seem real.

"Well, *I* think they're going to come and get us out pretty soon," said Blossom. "I mean, they have to. I don't deserve to be here. That other girl, Lola, thinks they're just going to leave us here, and maybe that's what they're going to do to *her*, but—"

"But she might be right," Abigail interrupted, turning from Blossom to look Oliver briefly in the eye. "It couldn't be a mistake, it's all too crazy and coincidental. Don't you think so? I'm really kind of scared. It's so . . . uncomfortable here, and who knows what might happen next? What . . . what do you think?"

"I don't think anything yet," said Oliver. "Who can think in this place?" He looked casually over his shoulder at the empty space below him. "But it sure beats solid geometry by a mile, I can tell you that!"

"But," said Peter, "but what if . . . what if they leave us here for a long time? I . . . I don't think I could stand it. I mean . . . I mean, there's nothing to lean against, nothing that feels safe. I just can't stop thinking that . . that. . . ." He stopped.

Abigail had never heard him say so much at one time.

"Stop thinking what?" Oliver said. "Come on, you can tell us."

"I . . . thinking that I'm going to fall," said Peter, and looked down at his feet.

"Yeah, and who isn't?" said Oliver. "But you're not going to fall unless you want to—or unless somebody pushes you, and I don't *think* I'm going to push you. And I don't think these girls want to push you either, do they?"

"I wouldn't mind pushing Lola," Blossom murmured.

"Say, where is this Lola, anyway?" Oliver asked.

"She went to find a toilet," said Abigail. "She thought if there was a food machine, there would probably be a toilet somewhere. And water. It makes sense. Somebody should have gone with her, I guess, but I was so tired of walking around."

Oliver was watching her. "And what's your name?" he asked.

"Abigail." She forced herself not to look away from him.

"And I'm Blossom."

"Blossom, huh. And my buddy there, what's your name?" He was still watching Abigail. When no answer came from Peter, he looked over at his face.

"Peter."

"Uh-huh. So it's Oliver, Abigail, Peter, Blossom, and—don't tell me—Lola!"

He was making it all seem like a game. Abigail couldn't understand how he could be so jaunty about the situation, but she was beginning to accept it, to drift with the mood he was creating. Peter, after his brief look of despair, now seemed more alert than he had ever been, gazing at Oliver in that doglike way. And Blossom now seemed to be relaxing. Abigail sensed that he met with her approval.

"Yes, Lola," Blossom sighed. "If only she wasn't here! Everybody else is nice."

For a moment no one spoke. Abigail wished Blossom would stop talking that way, it was embarrassing, and so pointless.

"Well anyway," Oliver said, "here we all are. We might as well enjoy ourselves while we're waiting."

"Well, maybe we should try to make the food thing work," said Blossom. "Maybe it would work for Oliver."

"Sure, why shouldn't it?" said Oliver. "They don't want to starve us. Actually, I think it's kind of fun here, like a dream in a video show. We should probably all be dancing and singing." He stood up suddenly and jumped down to the landing. Spreading his arms, he began to sing, smiling at each of them as he turned in a small circle. "Just singin' my cares away," he sang. "On the happy little steppy steps. Just singin' till my heart goes—" He stopped suddenly and reached out for Abigail's hand, pulling her to her feet. "Come on, you too," he said, swinging her arm and swaying back and forth. "Let's give them a little show."

Abigail had never been touched by a boy before, and though she felt a bit frightened and embarrassed, nevertheless the pressure and warmth of his hand were strangely thrilling. And he began singing again, funny nonsense words that made them all laugh, that made Abigail almost forget where they were.

chapter 6

Their voices, when Lola heard them at last, meant that
something strange was going on, that much she could tell
as she made her way up the spiral flight. (Somehow she
had ended up below them.) There was a lot of chatter, as
though they were all talking at once, and laughter. The
nerve of them, laughing! She had been thinking hard as
she wandered, and was in no mood for laughter herself.
Even Peter seemed to be talking a lot. Or singing. The un-
likelihood of Peter singing was what made her begin to
think that there was an unfamiliar male up there, and that
he was singing.

She stopped just below the hole. "Happy little sunshine,
baby boo," came the singing voice. "Gurgily goo, Boppity
boo. Strange flowers, growing in my garden of love, my
garden of love love love." Mystified, Lola took a deep
breath and stuck her head through. It was a new boy all
right, and good-looking, she supposed, in a kind of chis-
eled and yet puckish way. He was shamelessly showing

41

off, singing some stupid song, and they were all adoring him. Especially Abigail, who was standing beside him and actually holding his hand. It was awful, grimly watching them have fun, feeling out of it, but afraid to interrupt and spoil it all.

But he noticed her right away. "Lola!" he said, stopping suddenly. "It *is* Lola, isn't it? Welcome to the funny farm."

In two bounds she was up on the landing, standing an inch away from him, and glaring up into his eyes. He was at least four inches taller than she, and grinning at her in this maddening way. "Yes, it is Lola," she said, "and this *must* be the funny farm. What the hell's going on?"

"We were just having fun," Blossom piped up in her nasal whine. "There's nothing wrong with that."

Lola put her hands on her hips. "Who said there was anything—"

"Yeah," said the boy, turning his head to look at Blossom. "She didn't say there was anything wrong." Blossom glared at him, but he didn't seem to notice, turning back to Lola. "I've been working," he explained good-humoredly. "Entertaining them. Keeping their spirits up."

Lola looked quickly around at the others. All the laughter had gone out of the situation. "Oh," she said, still an inch away from him. She wanted to say something slightly nasty, for it wasn't very pleasant to have ruined their fun. She felt like an old grouch. "Oh," she said again, and looked down; then she slipped quickly past him and over to the empty stairs across from Blossom. She sat down and lit a cigarette, forcing herself not to notice how few were left.

"So why the silence?" said the new boy, turning from

one to the other of them and shrugging slightly. "Why the long faces? We were having fun."

"Why don't you ask Lola?" said Blossom. "She's the one who ruined it."

That did it. "Yes, why don't you ask Lola?" Lola said, ripping the cigarette from her lips. "Ask Lola, because she knows; she knows where we are. If any of you spent one second using your feeble brains to think about it, you'd know it too. We're in a prison, do you realize that? A prison. And it's not just an ordinary prison, it's a torture chamber. Get that? A torture chamber. But it doesn't torture our bodies, it doesn't do easy, obvious little things like pulling off our arms and legs or sticking red-hot knives under our fingernails. Oh, no. It's worse. It's supposed to make us go insane, don't you realize?" She waved her cigarette over her head. "All these stupid stairs going nowhere, no flat place, no walls, nowhere to hide, no way to get out, no explanation. Don't you realize? They made it on purpose, it's all for us, they're *doing* something to us. It's so obvious. And you sit around laughing and singing stupid songs. Think about it." She paused for breath. They were all staring at her as if she really were insane. "And," she went on, "and . . . oh, hell! And I found a toilet. And I guess we've gotta drink out of it too. I couldn't find any other water."

For a moment no one spoke. The new boy's face had loosened, the high color draining from his cheeks; but almost at once he pulled it back together, looking at her now with angry determination, and no humor at all.

Abigail spoke first. "A toilet? You really found one?"

"Yes," said Lola proudly, partly mollified. "And wouldn't you know, it's right in the middle of one of those lousy

43

bridges. The worst place it could be. Don't you see what that means? Doesn't it tell you something? Why are we being forced to drink out of it, why in hell should it be *there*, except to be unpleasant and frightening to us?"

"I—I guess you're right," said Abigail. "I'm sure you're right, there's no other explanation. But we . . . for a minute we forgot. For a minute, we were almost having fun. That's all."

"I know," Lola said less fiercely. "I'm sorry. I didn't want to spoil it. But I was so upset about all this."

"So what? Other people get upset too," the new boy said. He was still standing, staring at her. "That doesn't give you the right to criticize what we were doing. You act like you think you're pretty tough, but you're just as hysterical as any other girl. We don't have to listen to it."

He was her adversary now, she could tell. And she had done it herself, just as she had done with Blossom. Silently, she cursed herself. It was so stupid, opening her big mouth like that and making him hate her; it was just going to make everything worse. But maybe it wasn't too late. Even though "hysterical" still rankled, Abigail's recognition had calmed her down to the point where she could swallow her pride. "I know," she said. "I shouldn't have gotten so mad. But it was frustrating. Nobody seemed to understand how serious this was. But," and she let her pride sink down to the bottom of her stomach, "but what you were doing was a good thing, I guess. I'm sorry I said it was stupid. It's," she sighed, "it's important to keep people in a good mood."

The boy grunted, turning from her to the food machine. "Oh," she said. "Did anybody make it work?"

"No," Blossom said pettishly. "And nobody even wanted to try."

"Well, I'm ready now," said the new boy. "Suddenly I'm starving."

And they tried. One by one, each of them struggled over the unresponsive screen while the others watched impatiently, growing hungrier and hungrier, waiting and hoping for the whirs and the clicks that would not come. And at last they grew tired of it, and quietly, one by one, they retreated to their respective stairways, Oliver sitting above Peter. They sat for a while, too dispirited to speak; until at last their eyes began to close.

chapter 7

When she awoke, Blossom could not remember for a moment where she was. There was a gleaming whiteness, and something sharp pressing painfully into her back. But most strange and disturbing of all was the terrible emptiness inside herself, the emptiness that she could not bear. She had to make the hunger go away.

And then it all came back to her: the blindfold, the stairways, hating Lola, everything. Hating Lola: She clung to that. Hating was so vital, so necessary. It was even her *duty*, in fact, to probe into Lola's odiousness, and to help the others, for their own good, to understand it.

Lola opened her eyes and sat up. "Mmm," she said thickly.

Oliver sat up and stretched. "Hello, everybody." He yawned. "So we're still here, huh?"

Abigail was still trying to sleep, curled up against the steps, her eyes closed. Peter's eyes were closed too, his chin resting against his chest.

Blossom was beginning to feel something else, almost as uncomfortable as the hunger. It was horrible having to ask Lola for help, but there was really no alternative. "Uh," she said. "Um, I have to—I mean, how do you get to . . . you know, what you found . . .?"

"Oh, yeah," Lola said. "The toilet. I suppose you want to know where it is."

"Well, you're the only one who knows."

"Well, okay." Lola looked around. "Anybody else want to come?"

"I think I'll stick around and watch over the sleeping beauties here," said Oliver. "You can tell me how to get there later. I'll be able to find it. And maybe I'll try to get this thing here working again."

"Well, come on then," Lola mumbled, and they started off.

Lola moved quickly. Soon Blossom was out of breath. Her thighs rubbed together stickily, and her skirt, which was beginning to feel dirty, flapped irritatingly around her knees. And Lola was far ahead now, making Blossom feel clumsy and slow.

And then Lola stopped at a landing ahead. She looked from side to side, as if trying to decide which way to go. Blossom hurried to catch up with her. She was panting and her forehead was damp when she reached the landing. Lola still had not moved.

"What's the matter?" Blossom said, gasping for breath. "Did you already forget where it is?"

"No, I did *not* forget," said Lola, turning to her. "I'm just trying to decide which is the best way to go. And you can find it yourself if you don't like the way I'm doing it. I'm getting pretty sick of your attitude. Why are you always picking at me? What have you got against me anyway?"

"I—" Blossom began. She had to be careful. Now she knew it had been a mistake to make it so obvious to Lola that she hated her. She had to undo that now, for only if Lola trusted her would she have the necessary power over her. "I just . . . when you first came along, you scared me, and you were mean. That's all."

Lola slapped herself on the forehead and rolled up her eyes. "You still thinking about that? How long does it take you to forget something stupid like that?"

I never forget, thought Blossom.

"I mean, I already told you, I was just worried about the food," Lola went on. "By now you should know the way I talk. It didn't mean anything." She shook her head. "You know, we're in a pretty tricky spot as it is. You're just making it worse."

"I . . . I guess you're right," said Blossom, making an effort to sound contrite. "I never really meant it, really. I just didn't want you to boss me around."

"Mmm," said Lola, her eyes probing. "Sure that's all it was?"

"Yes," Blossom nodded quickly, pursing her lips. "I'm sure."

"Well, let's hope it's all over with now. I won't stand for much more of it."

"I . . . I know you wouldn't stand for it," Blossom said softly. "I guess I was just waiting for you to tell me to stop."

"Well, now I'm telling you. And I'll tell you something else. Somebody's got to get bossed around here, you better get used to it, because somebody's got to be the leader.

If there's no leader, we'll never get anywhere. I'm not saying the leader's gotta be *me*, necessarily, but there's gotta be one."

Now that her breath and her wits were back, Blossom rose to Lola's opening. "Oh, but I think it *should* be you," Blossom said. "Who else could be the leader? Not Peter, and not Abigail, and not *me*. That just leaves you and Oliver. And, well, Oliver. . . ."

"Yeah?" said Lola. "Well Oliver what?"

"I just think he's sort of strange," Blossom said thoughtfully, twisting a ringlet. "The way he was dancing around like that, singing those stupid songs and things. . . ."

"You looked like you were enjoying it." Lola was squinting at her suspiciously.

"Well, yesss." *Careful now*, Blossom told herself.

"In fact you were the one who defended him, if I remember it right."

"But I was still mad at *you* then," said Blossom. "Now I—"

"Don't you have to go to the toilet?" said Lola, turning around. "It's this way." And she started up the stairs.

Blossom felt like kicking her. She just *had* to find something she could use to turn the others against her.

Ahead, Lola bent over and picked something up from a step. It looked like a scrap of cloth. Lola waited, whistling through her teeth, and she actually turned and smiled at Blossom when she reached her.

"We're almost there now," Lola said, sounding pleased with herself. "See this? I tore it off my shirt and left it here yesterday, as a marker."

"Oh," said Blossom. It had been a clever thing to do in this confusing place, though it annoyed her to have to

49

acknowledge any virtue in her enemy. Nevertheless, remembering her role, she said, "That was smart of you. I never would have thought of it."

"To tell you the truth, I almost didn't myself. In fact—" Watching Blossom's face, Lola's smile quickly faded. "But I would have found the way without it," she added, her voice guarded again. "I'm gonna leave it here for the others."

She still doesn't trust me, Blossom said to herself, following her upward again. *I've got to get her to trust me. But how?*

And in the end she succeeded, though not without a sacrifice.

The toilet, as Lola had said, was on a narrow bridge, just a small round hole filled with water, flushing constantly. It was difficult to get to, even more difficult for Blossom to drink from it, and then squat there, teetering and clutching at the bridge, while she used it. And embarrassing; for though Lola seemed to be staring politely off in the other direction, when Blossom looked back at her to check she was almost sure she saw Lola quickly turning away, a smirk on her face, as though she had been watching her and laughing. It was infuriating. And when she herself, overcoming her natural repugnance in order to pay Lola back, turned to spy on *her* sitting there, Lola just waved and cried out, "Enjoying the view?"

But Lola grew more serious as they started to leave. "Hey, listen," she said. "Those other guys are gonna have trouble finding this place, even with that marker I left. It might be good if we left something here, so they could tell from below which bridge it was. And I don't really have anything to leave, I've already torn up my shirt. But maybe, well . . . well one of those ruffles on your dress, if we could hang it down over the bridge, it would be real easy to see from far away."

Her dress? But it was her favorite dress. It was unthinkable. How could this hateful girl even suggest it? Her voice shrill, Blossom began to shout. "They can find it anyway! Why should I—"

Lola's expression stopped her. She was nodding, her lips pursed, her eyes sliding off to the side. It was just as if she were saying, *I knew you'd say that, you trivial, selfish thing*. With a tremendous effort, Blossom forced herself to think rationally. There was no way of avoiding it; she had to tear off that ruffle. Not only was it a matter of principle to show Lola that she was wrong about her, but if she didn't make this sacrifice now, Lola would probably never trust her. Breathing heavily, Blossom picked up the hem of her skirt. Hardly able to watch her hands, she pulled the bottom ruffle off all the way around the skirt. She stepped out of it, and staring hard at Lola (who was watching her as though she couldn't believe her eyes), ripped apart its one seam, turning it from a circle into a long strip. "Here," she said wheezily, and handed Lola the piece of cloth.

For a moment Lola seemed confused. She stood there, the cloth dangling from her hand, still just watching Blossom with her head tilted to the side, squinting. "You know," she said at last, "I never thought you'd do that."

"I . . . I didn't want to," Blossom said, pleased with Lola's reaction. "But what you said was right. And what does a dress matter in here anyway?" With what she hoped was a sad little gesture, she picked up her ruined hem and gazed wistfully at it.

"It'll be a big help," Lola said. "It really will. Everybody will appreciate it." She turned away quickly, ran out along the bridge, and tied one end of the cloth around it, so that it hung several feet below, motionless in the still air.

After that, Blossom got what she needed with hardly any trouble at all.

chapter 8

They had been up for hours now, and had been working at the machine, on and off, for the entire time. They were hungry, not having eaten since the previous afternoon, and getting more and more irritable. And still the machine refused to respond.

"Stubborn bitch!" Oliver said. He was out of breath, sweat was dripping from his nose, and his T-shirt clung stickily to his chest. Struggling over the machine without any breakfast, without even having brushed his teeth, was not very enjoyable. Yet he had forced himself to keep on trying. It was not only that he was hungrier than he had ever been in his life; he also desperately wanted to be the one to make the machine work. Somehow his relationship to all the others depended on it.

"Using dirty words isn't going to do any good," said Blossom peevishly. She was hunched over at the bottom of her stairway, staring intensely down at the machine.

"Well then you try again," Oliver said, wiping his forehead with the back of his hand and sitting down. He watched the fat girl bend over the screen for the hundredth time and stick out her tongue at it. He felt like hooting at her, for she looked ridiculous; but though she was a cow, there was something about her that made him feel he should watch his step with her.

Lola sat tensely on her step, biting her thumbnail as she watched Blossom. Every once in a while her hand would move toward her shirt pocket and the pack of cigarettes, then quickly back to her mouth again. She was unlike any girl Oliver had ever known (he hadn't known very many), and made him feel slightly uneasy, for she did not respond to him the way other girls had. He felt no power over her, no ability to make her stammer and blush by merely smiling at her, and for this reason he did not know how to behave with her. He also didn't like it that she had been the one to find the toilet. It put her altogether too much in the leadership position, the position he craved for himself. That was why he felt it had to be he who made the food machine work, and that was why he was beginning to resent Lola.

At least there were Abigail and Peter! With Abigail he thought he knew where he stood; she acted just the way he expected girls to behave. And furthermore, here they were without any adults around! He had never been alone with a girl, and the thought of what might possibly happen was terribly exciting—though also a little frightening.

He shifted on the step, and Peter looked up at him for a moment, wide-eyed. It had been rather unexpected to find himself almost at once the object of Peter's intense devotion, but Oliver didn't mind. It made him feel confident and powerful to have someone look up to him so much. Although, down at the bottom of it, something about Peter gnawed at him.

He shook his head, smiling to himself, trying to laugh at and discard the discomforting fact that there wasn't one of them that didn't bother him in some small way. What was it that Lola had been shouting about yesterday? That they were in a prison, that they were being tortured and driven mad? It was a bit farfetched; but on the other hand, it might just be possible that each of them had been picked for a certain reason. . . .

He shook his head again, looking down at Abigail and smiling. He wasn't used to thinking this way, and didn't enjoy it.

Abigail smiled back, rather wanly.

At that moment Blossom turned toward them, noticing his expression. "Are you laughing at me?" she demanded, getting up from the floor and plumping down on her step. "How dare you laugh at me? Here I am, trying to make this thing work, while you sit there, laughing and jeering and—"

"No, no!" Oliver waved her down. "Come on, calm down. I was only smiling at Abigail. Can't a guy even smile?"

"What's there to smile about?" said Lola. "We're trapped in this prison and now that food thing won't even work." She gestured at it contemptuously. "It was just teasing us before, making us expect something and then taking it away. And I'm having a cigarette!" she added defiantly, taking out the pack and quickly lighting one.

"Who said you couldn't? Oliver asked her. "We're not hallway patrolmen."

"Oh, who said you were?" said Lola tiredly.

Oliver couldn't stand it any longer. He wanted to get away from all the frustration and the bickering. He wanted to get away with Abigail. "Come on, Abigail," he said rather awkwardly, hardly daring to hope that she would have the nerve to go off with him. "Um . . . maybe we should go look around. There might be another food machine somewhere that works."

Abigail looked down. "Oh . . . ," she murmured. She waited for a moment. "Um . . . well, all right," she said at last, standing up and smiling nervously. She blushed.

"Well, come on then," he said quickly. Now that she had agreed, he wanted to get her away as soon as possible, before anyone else could offer to come along. "Let's go." He jumped down to the landing and onto her stairway, pushing her lightly on the back. Without looking at the others, they started up.

Abigail continued to seem embarrassed, looking down at her feet as they climbed. Obviously she had never been alone with a boy before. There was nothing unusual about that, of course; boys and girls were kept strictly segregated in all state institutions. As they grew into their teens they would sometimes have classes together in order to get used to one another; but they had all been taught from their earliest years about the dangers of mixing too freely with the opposite sex. It was immoral to get very intimate with anyone, unless you were about to be married.

Still, people have feelings, and do not always agree with everything they are taught. Though Abigail seemed a bit apprehensive, her very acceptance of his invitation was enough to tell Oliver that she might be interested in trying what was forbidden. The thought of it set his heart beating quickly; yet he had no idea what he should do.

"But . . . but what *is* going to happen to us?" Abigail said at last. "Yesterday you thought this was all like a game, but I bet you don't anymore."

He looked down into her worried face, feeling a new and unknown kind of excitement flowing from her helplessness. It was true that he no longer thought it was a game, and was actually rather frightened about the situation. But the last thing he would do was admit his real feelings to her: His strength depended upon feeling superior.

"Don't get upset," he said. "It'll be okay. Please." They had reached a small landing, and stopped walking.

"I usually don't get upset," Abigail said, her eyes on the ground. "I'm usually calm. Most people I know . . . think I don't have any emotions, because I don't show them very much. But I do have them. And sometimes . . . they're very strong."

"I . . . I can tell that," Oliver said in a hoarse whisper. The situation was becoming almost too much to bear, being alone with a girl and talking about something as intimate as her emotions. He was breathing heavily now; and when Abigail suddenly looked up at him, her face close to his and her eyes very wide, all at once something inside him took over. It didn't matter now that he didn't know what to do; of its own accord his hand reached out and grasped hers, and he bent down his head and kissed her on the lips.

Oh, it was strange, thrilling and strange! The touch of lips was new to him, and the sensation of it rang throughout his body. Her lips were hard at first, and dry; but then they softened, and parted slightly, and she fell against him, her free hand draping across his back.

In a moment Oliver broke away, besieged all at once by

57

a totally different set of feelings. There was shame; shame and acute embarrassment at having done something so intimate and so wrong. But more than that there was a kind of terrible responsibility. What did it mean to this girl that he had touched her that way? What would she expect from him now? And would he be able to live up to her expectations? She was watching him, startled by his sudden pulling away; and from her parted lips and dazed, half-closed eyes, he sensed that she would still like to be kissing. Abruptly he turned from her.

"What's wrong?" said Abigail. "Did I do something wrong? Oliver! What is it? Say something, please."

He closed his eyes and shook his head.

"But . . . but I thought you wanted to. You started it. They always said boys wouldn't respect girls who . . . did that, but I thought it would be different in here. Oh, Oliver, please tell me what's wrong!"

"I . . . maybe we should go look around," he said, still not looking at her. "Maybe there's another food machine."

After that, she stopped asking. They wandered slowly for an hour or so, not speaking, avoiding one another's eyes. And as they wandered, Oliver began thinking again of the touch of her lips, of her arm against his back; and as those memories became more intense, the shame and fear began to be forgotten. Soon he felt like kissing her again.

"Abigail," he said, stopping in the middle of a flight.

She turned to him with a melancholic, resigned expression. "Could we go back now?" she said. "Maybe something happened back there."

"All right." He sighed, searching for words. "But . . . I just want to say, I'm sorry if I acted funny." He paused again. He couldn't tell her his real reasons: There was something unmanly about them. "It has nothing to do with you. It just . . . reminded me of something."

"Are you sure?" Abigail said. "Because I got the distinct feeling you didn't like me. You don't have to like me, you know. I don't want you being *nice* to me, unless you really mean it."

"I do like you," he insisted, suddenly wanting the conversation to end. "But we better get back to the others. Come on."

They started down. But suddenly she gave a little cry, and stopped. Below them, a red light was flashing on and off, glinting against the white surfaces. And all at once the air was filled with whispering voices.

chapter 9

"I hope they hurry up and bring back some food," Blossom said, twisting her hands as she watched Oliver and Abigail disappear into the whiteness above. "It must be way past lunchtime by now."

"I wonder if food is really what they're after?" Lola mused.

"What do you mean by that?"

"Oh, I don't know. Haven't you ever wondered what it might be like to be alone with a boy?"

"What?" Blossom was shocked. "You mean. . . . But that's immoral and dangerous! Didn't they ever tell you that? Why—"

Peter closed his eyes. He wasn't interested in their conversation, which, being naïve, he didn't understand anyway. He wanted to think about Oliver. Basically, it was like having Jasper back again.

But no sooner had that thought entered his mind than another came and quickly contradicted it. It really wasn't like having Jasper back again, it was very, very different. His delight began to fade. It disturbed him, for instance, to see Oliver go off with Abigail. He would even have braved the steps and bridges to be with Oliver, but clearly Oliver hadn't wanted him to come, and the rejection was quite painful.

It had never been like that with Jasper . . . Jasper . . . The old home. The room they had shared. The pictures came easily to his mind now, and they had undergone a change. The walls of the room swayed with rainbow colors, and the furniture seemed to be alive, each object with its own benevolent personality, murmuring comforting words to him, enclosing and protecting him. He let himself drift into it, cradled in the warm, underwater, rainbow-hued dimness that undulated around him.

But suddenly there was something in the way. Something harsh and irritating. He tried to push it away, but it would not go. Something was flashing on and off, and there were strange sounds, and a girl screaming. Reluctantly he opened his eyes.

It was the food machine. Its screen, which usually glowed dully, was now flashing on and off with an intense, bright red light, so bright that it dazzled his eyes. And all around them were invisible, whispering voices, saying something indistinct that he could not understand.

Blossom was hysterical, jumping up and down and pointing to the machine. "What's it doing? What's it doing?" she shrieked, stopping to stick out her tongue frantically. "Maybe it's going to work now, maybe it will work, how can we make it work?"

Lola, who had leaped to her feet, was oddly enough staring at Peter. "Peter," she murmured, in a strangely hushed voice, "Peter, what's the matter with you? You've been sitting there staring at that blinking light for more than a minute and you didn't even notice it."

"What?" he mumbled. "Staring? But . . . but I was asleep, dreaming. My eyes were closed."

She was standing motionless, watching him. "They were open," she said, her voice still hushed. "They were wide open, Peter, your eyes were open the whole time."

"Who cares about his eyes?" Blossom shrieked. "What are those voices saying? Maybe they're telling us what to do. Maybe they're telling us how to work the machine! We've got to do something!"

"How . . . how long ago did the others leave?" Peter asked, ignoring Blossom. A prickling of fear was crawling up the back of his neck. It seemed to him that they had left about fifteen minutes ago, and that the light had been flashing for only a few seconds.

"They left a couple of hours ago," Lola answered, still staring at him.

"Why are you just standing there?" cried Blossom. "*Do* something, this might be our only chance!"

What *were* the voices saying? Peter wondered as he got to his feet, trying not to think about what Lola had just told him. They seemed to be saying the same thing over and over again, but the different voices were not speaking in unison, and the individual words were blurred and indistinct. It was like a hundred people with cotton in their mouths, whispering the same thing at different times.

"I know!" Blossom cried. "They're saying, 'Food will be coming soon. Food will be coming soon.' Listen, can't you hear it?" Her eyes were darting wildly, and she clasped her hands together. "Oh, I hope they're right, I hope they're telling the truth! It's been so long since we've had any food."

"Shhh!" said Lola, waving her hand at Blossom. "I'm just getting it. . . . And you're wrong," she went on suddenly. "That's not what they're saying at all. They're saying 'Nude in the house of the doomed.' It's obvious."

"But why would they say *that*?" Blossom cried shrilly. "It's meaningless." She spun around to Peter. "You can hear it too. They're saying, 'Food will be coming soon.' Aren't they? Aren't they?"

Peter shook his head. "I . . . It, it sounds like . . . 'Be careful in Oliver's room.'"

"*What*?" cried Blossom. "But you're both wrong. They're saying—"

"They're saying 'Nude in the house of the doomed,'" Lola insisted. "Because that's what we are. We're helpless in this crazy place. Or at least they want us to *think* we're helpless. You just think it's food because that's all you ever think about."

"Stop *saying* things like that!" Blossom shouted, stamping her foot. "Stop being mean to me! Just remember, you said a couple of things this morning that I could always tell a few certain—"

"What?" Lola stepped toward her. "What the hell are you talking about, you—"

She was interrupted by voices from above, and hurrying footsteps. "—it isn't," Oliver was saying. "Can't you hear them? They're saying, 'She gobbled him up in the womb.'"

"No, it's 'The dish ran away with the spoon,'" said Abigail, sounding out of breath. "It really is, Oliver."

Lola turned back to Blossom, stepping menacingly

toward her. Blossom took a step back. "What the hell did you mean about—"

For a moment they were all in motion: Lola moving toward Blossom, and Blossom backing away; Oliver jumping to the landing and Abigail, shaking her head, coming down a step behind him; Peter moving forward, almost involuntarily, to greet Oliver. And in that moment there was a whir and a click from the floor, clearly audible above the whispers rustling around them.

Five hungry pairs of eyes focused instantly on the slot beside the blinking light. And out of the slot rolled a tiny ball, not a cylinder; a tiny ball hardly big enough for one small bite.

They all started toward it at once.

"Stop!" shouted Lola. And there was such urgency and command in her voice that they did stop. "Wait! Don't move. Listen." She was breathing heavily. "Stay where you are. One of us just did something that made it work. Nobody knows what it is, right?"

They nodded silently.

"So stay right where you are and do what you were just doing. That's the only way to figure it out. And don't grab the food! Wait till we know how to make it work!"

Lola stepped toward Blossom again, Blossom backed away (not without a glance of longing at the little ball on the floor); Oliver went quickly back up to his step and jumped down, Abigail shook her head behind him; and Peter moved toward him again.

And nothing happened.

"Again!" Lola cried. "*Exactly* like the first time!"

The voices whispering around them, echoing through vast white spaces. The red light blinking in steady rhythm, falling rhythmically back at them from above in hundreds of pieces, so that they could not help but move in time with it. Now they were all watching each other, timing their movements to each other as well as the blinking light.

And there was a whir and a click and another little ball rolling onto the landing.

"Again!" Lola cried. "*Exactly* like the first time!"

It was at this moment that it became a dance. Lola and Blossom facing each other, moving away from the light, then back at each whir and click, and away again to bring on another; Oliver jumping down to the landing, and Abigail shaking her head behind him; and Peter each time moving toward Oliver, then away again, watching the red light flashing on Oliver's cheekbones, Abigail a vague, moving shadow behind him.

Blossom, of course, was the one who broke it.

"No!" she gasped, pushing Lola aside with her outstretched hand at the beginning of another repetition, and she pounced at the little pile of brown balls. "I'm too hungr—" and her mouth was full.

At this, the others pounced too, even Peter. For a moment it was a wild free-for-all, pushing and grabbing, all of them out of breath. Somehow no one got pushed off the landing, and everyone got at least a few bites, but only enough to have a very mild effect on their hunger, although Blossom got more than the others. The meat was just as delicious as it had been before.

When there was no more left, Lola backed away from the others, wiping her mouth with the back of her hand. "You sure botched that one," she said, still panting slightly.

"Who, me?" said Blossom, looking up at her from where she was kneeling on the floor, scraping up a bit of food that had been flattened under someone's shoe.

"Yes, you!" The whispering and the flashing light were still going on, but as Lola took out her next to last cigarette, they both stopped, quite suddenly. The stillness was startling.

"Well, you don't have to look at me like that," Blossom retorted, filling the silence with her whine. "We did figure it out. We can always do it again."

"Can we?" Lola said, blowing out smoke. "Who says so? The other time it worked, doing the same thing didn't make it work again. Why should it be any different now?"

"But . . . ," said Blossom.

"We should have kept going until it stopped on its own, and saved some food for later," Lola went on. "That would have been the only sensible—"

"Oh, leave her alone," said Oliver, in a voice so uncharacteristically irritable that it sent a small shock through Peter's body. Oliver retreated to Abigail's stairway and sat down beside her. "We got enough to eat. Stop bitching."

"Maybe *you* got enough," Lola said, rubbing her shoulder. "I can still feel it where you pushed me away. God *damn*, I wish I were stronger than you!"

"Please," Abigail said. "Stop fighting, please. Look, we did get some food, we should be glad about it. And maybe it will work again. We won't know until we try."

Which they did. They tried, awkwardly and with the embarrassment that, due to the excitement, had been missing before. And it did not work.

"I told you so," Lola said, when they had given up.

"Now we're going to have to figure out something else to do."

"Not now," Abigail said. "Please. I'm exhausted. We've been up for a long time, I want to get some sleep."

And so, with a kind of relief, Peter returned to the magic room, where everything was beautiful and strange, and where effort and pain, and stairways, did not exist.

chapter 10

Abigail and Peter had no trouble getting to sleep but it was quite awhile before Blossom and Oliver dropped off, and Lola was the last of all. She was also the first to wake when, about fifteen minutes after she had finally dozed off, the whispers and the flashing light began again.

"Nude in the house of the doomed. Nude in the house of the doomed," whispered hundreds of invisible voices on all sides of her, as Lola sat up, rubbing her eyes and trying to decide if she really had to wake them all. Yes, she decided, she did have to. It was too important an opportunity to miss, for perhaps their dance would work now, as it had the other time the whispering and the flashing light had come.

Abigail was surprisingly difficult to wake up, and Peter was nearly impossible. It was only after Oliver shook him roughly for nearly a minute, shouting in his ear, that he finally opened his eyes, murmuring, and not seeming to see any of them.

The dance did not go well at first. They were stumbling and dull-witted, and Lola was in a hurry, for there was no way of knowing how long the special conditions would last. But finally they did get into the rhythm of it, remembering, in their hunger, their precise movements from before. And it worked.

It went on for about ten minutes; and when the light and the whispering stopped, so did the food. They had earned a rather substantial pile, but even Lola made no attempt to put any aside for later. They devoured it instantly.

And so they learned the first rudiments of their dance, and that they were to be told when to perform it. It was not long before they learned as well that the machine was a capricious provider, for even with the flashing light and the whispers and the dance, it did not always work. Nevertheless, it fed them often enough, and kept them hungry enough, so that every time the whispers and the light began, they would instantly begin to dance, hoping that this time there would be food.

And of course, whether it worked or not was part of a pattern, and there would be other patterns too. But as yet they were too close to the outside world to be able to understand them, or to tolerate what was inevitably going to come.

part two

chapter 11

In the days that followed, they began to talk more freely. Of course they were still very uneasy about where they were and what was happening to them, but most of them were beginning to grow a little more accustomed to being there, and could occasionally think about something else.

"So I said, 'Listen, if you think you're so tough, prove it,'" Oliver said. "So we started circling each other."

"You mean you started to fight, right in the hall and everything?" Abigail asked with awe in her voice. "But what if a hallway patrolman came along?"

"I didn't care. I was furious. I wasn't going to let anybody push me around!"

"Yeah, and how about the video screens?" Lola said. "I suppose you managed to get out of range of them, huh?"

"I wasn't thinking about it," said Oliver, annoyed. "Anyway, so we start circling each other," he went on, trying to put back into the story the tension that Lola had broken, "and then suddenly he comes at me, and starts to hit me, and I give him a kick, just like on the video shows. I kicked out and knocked him down, and he just lay there, and gave up. And then I got out of there fast, and the wardens never found out it was me. He was too embarrassed to tell." He sat back confidently.

Lola shook her head. "Oh, sure. How about the video screens?" she said.

"But I can't stand it," Blossom moaned. "I can't *stand* it! Why didn't it work?"

For fifteen minutes they had been dancing in rhythm to the light with no result, until at last one, then another pellet had rolled out, and the light and the voices had suddenly stopped. Blossom and Oliver had each snatched one pellet; the others had nothing. It was unbearably frustrating, for not only were they hungry, but food was the only comforting thing there was, the one relief to everything harsh and barren and alien around them. To each of them, it had quickly become more important than anything else.

"I don't understand," Abigail said faintly. "We did it just the same the last time the light and voices came, and the time before that, and it worked both those times. It just doesn't make sense."

"And it wasn't even trying to make us change anything," said Oliver, shaking his head. "You know it always feeds us *first* when it wants us to change. And we *were* doing it exactly the same as last time, I know we were."

"Maybe there's some kind of pattern to it," said Lola. "I mean for when it works and when it doesn't."

"Oh, there is not," said Oliver. "It's completely unpredictable. The last two times it worked, the time before that it didn't work, like this time, then before that it worked, and before that it didn't work for two times. . . . Who can remember anyway? There's no pattern. It's just fickle."

"Machines aren't fickle," Lola said, turning away.

"And my best friend's father was the *director* of the whole International Industrial Conglomerates Lobbying Operation," said Blossom.

"Not that guy Edward Baker Jackson, who's always on video programs?" Oliver asked.

Blossom nodded. "*The* Edward Baker Jackson. My best friend's father. They lived in a house too, near ours. He was really a famous lobbyist, and brilliant, his operations were always successful. In fact my father used to say it was really him who—" She stopped and put her hand over her mouth.

"Who what?" said Lola.

Blossom thought for a moment. Yes, she decided, she could tell them that. She took her hand away from her mouth. "Well . . . well maybe it doesn't matter. I've already told you so much *really* classified stuff anyway. My father used to say it was really Mr. Jackson who ran the administration, that he had the President in the palm of his hand." Blossom looked around at them proudly, folding her arms across her chest. "And he was my best friend's father."

"Books?" Oliver said, amazed. "But why use a book? They're so slow, and most of them aren't even programmed."

Peter was embarrassed. "I . . . they just had some, at

this place where I was. . . . And, I kind of liked it. It felt like . . . like it was only talking to me, and . . . and I could go slow, if I wanted, without worrying about keeping up with the others."

"But really, that is kind of silly," Abigail tried to explain. "I mean a book is much less personal than a programmed screen that can respond to you according to your needs, and concentrate on what's hard for you, and go fast on what's easy. A book stays the same no matter *who's* reading it. And anyway, I don't see how anyone could read a whole long book, it must be so boring!"

"But . . . but it wasn't," Peter said faintly. "I . . . almost forgot I was reading it. The . . . the whole story was going on in my head." He stopped and looked down.

"I still don't understand," said Oliver. "I mean watching a real-life hologram right before your eyes is better than anything you could *imagine*."

"Hey!" Lola said, in the middle of the dance. "Look at the light! It's not red anymore, it's green!"

All but Blossom began to slow down.

"Don't stop!" Blossom shrieked. "Keep dancing! Who cares what color it is? What difference does it make?"

And she was right, it really didn't seem to make any difference; for they soon learned that the color of the light had no relation to whether or not the machine would give them food. Sometimes it would be red, sometimes green, and eventually they stopped wondering about it altogether.

Blossom watched Lola wandering far below them, exploring again, and her eyes were cold and sharp. She turned back to the others. "What good does she think it's going to do to go stupidly running around like that?" she said. "She just does it to get away from us, because she can't stand any of us. She thinks she's better than we are, doesn't she, Peter?" Blossom waited. "Peter! You know she thinks we're all stupid, tell them, you know she does."

Peter was looking down, twisting his hands. "I . . . I guess she said . . . I don't remember. . . ."

Blossom turned contemptuously away from him. "You don't remember anything. You don't even know what's going on half the time. But I remember. I remember what she said. And it wasn't pretty."

Oliver was watching her. She could see the interest in his eyes, even though he was pretending not to care. "Quite a few things," Blossom went on temptingly. "Interesting things. But not pretty. Not pretty at all. . . ."

"It was only an eight-lane road," said Lola. "But I was going pretty fast anyway, too fast, I guess. And I had the smog lights on and everything, but I could still only see about thirty feet ahead, even in the middle of the day. And it was an old road, so suddenly there was this curve ahead and before I knew it I was going off the edge. Sheesh!" She shook her head.

"But what happened?" said Abigail.

"Nothing. I mean the car was a total wreck, including the gas mask compartment, but I just opened the door and walked out of—"

"Next to the highway? You got out of the car next to the highway?" said Oliver, incredulous. "I thought you said the masks were smashed."

"They were. But in the first place it was a miracle I wasn't already dead. And then I kept going back to the car and sticking in my head to get the good air that was still left, and running back to the road and waving at the cars. It was a lucky day for me 'cause a cop car came by just as I thought I was gonna pass out. Took me right back to the home, of course. It was a long time before I tried anything like that again!"

Peter had gone away. His body sagged limply against the stairway like a half-stuffed toy, and his head hung grotesquely to the side, his mouth open. The sight of him frightened Lola. "Hey, Peter," she said. "Peter, wake up. Can't you hear me?"

"Oh, leave him alone," Oliver said sharply. "I'll wake him up when the time comes."

"But . . . but it doesn't seem right to let him get like that," Lola said. "He keeps doing it more and more. We should really try to stop him, or else sometime we might not be able to wake him up at all."

"How do you know?" said Oliver. "I've always been able to wake him up; I always will be able to. Leave him alone. He's happier the way he is."

"How do you know he is?" Lola asked.

"What difference does it make to you?" Oliver said, ending the conversation.

Lola was alternately grinding her teeth and chewing on her nails. It was always worse after they had eaten to be without a cigarette.

"Will you stop making that noise?" said Blossom. "It's driving me crazy."

"'Will you stop making that noise?'" Lola mimicked her in falsetto. "'Will you stop making that noise?' And for Christ sake will you leave me alone! You'd grind your teeth too! God damn this place, God damn that machine. Why the hell can't it give us cigarettes?" She stood up angrily.

"Oh, calm down," said Oliver. The good humor in his voice was wearing thin, and his words rang falsely. "They've got to come and get us pretty soon."

"Yes," Blossom said fervently. "They've got to come. Any time now."

"Sure," said Lola sarcastically. "Sure. They'll come and take us off to fairyland. And I'm a purple monkey. And I am goddam *sick* of listening to all this garbage. Nobody's gonna come and you all know it!" She turned and ran furiously up the stairs.

chapter **12**

As the weeks went by, Abigail began to grow envious of Lola. She never would have expected it of herself, because it was clear that in the real world Lola was an outsider, and being an outsider was one thing Abigail couldn't bear. Nevertheless she did envy Lola, for one specific reason: Lola's independence.

Early every morning (morning being when they woke up; no one had any idea now what time of day it was outside), while the rest of them were still groggily rousing themselves, Lola would be jogging briskly up to the toilet and back. And at what seemed to be the same time later each day, Lola would jog briskly down the stairs to some undisclosed point, and right back up again. It didn't seem to affect her when the others ridiculed or resented her for it. She would simply say, "I need my exercise," and that would be that.

What impressed Abigail was that Lola never did things just because other people wanted her to; Lola did what *she* wanted to do. To Abigail, who was always considering what boys thought of her, or what the other girls in her group would think, who was always trying to avoid doing whatever might hurt someone, or make her disliked, Lola's behavior was hard to understand. It made Abigail, in some strange way, feel trapped; trapped, and then resentful of Lola's freedom.

"There she goes again, like clockwork," Oliver said one afternoon as Lola bounded off down the stairs. "If any of us had watches we could set them by her."

"But I should think you would want to get some exercise too," said Abigail. "Didn't you always like sports?"

"Yes, yes, I liked sports," he said impatiently, and looked away from her. Abigail was stung. She turned to Blossom.

In what seemed like the three or four weeks that they had been there, Blossom was already beginning to change. Though she was still obese, the meager, irregular meals and the strenuous exercise of the dance were beginning to tell: Her dress was growing loose, and her face, even with its remaining puffiness, was taking on a grayish, pinched expression. But she did not seem at all pleased to be losing weight. They were always hungry, for the machine only fed them enough to keep going, never enough to satisfy; and Blossom took this constant deprivation the hardest, often bending hopefully over the machine, rocking slightly, twisting her hands and pursing her lips.

Peter was growing stranger too. More and more now he would lapse into dazes, in which he would be utterly distant and unreachable, as though deserted by a mind that had flown miles and miles away. And it was difficult to get him to take his part in the food dance. Only Oliver could bring him out of the daze, and often it took time. More than once they had finally managed to get him moving, only to have the voices and the flashing light stop a moment later, taking away the possibility of food. This had not pleased any of them; Blossom, in a frenzy, had even slapped Peter once.

Abigail sighed. Oliver had changed too; or perhaps it wasn't as much a change as a peeling off of an outer layer. The confident energy and high spirits that had once characterized him were now only occasionally apparent. Instead he was often moody and petulant, and toward Lola even hostile. Somehow, Lola's energy seemed to drain his away, and, in lethargy, he hated her for it.

Nevertheless, Abigail was still attracted to him. He was probably the best-looking boy she had ever met, and the growing gauntness of his face only accentuated what was interesting about his features. He was often nasty to her, of course. Not infrequently now they would climb high above the others and kiss. Sometimes they would do it for as long as five minutes, and the kissing would grow more passionate. And even though she had always been taught that it was wrong, it was so comforting, and felt so nice, that she was beginning to think that the teaching might be wrong, not the act; and she was able to relax and enjoy it. But it would always end with Oliver suddenly breaking away, leaving her startled and lost, and after that he would be distant and cold.

She could not understand it, it was disturbing to think about, and so she turned her thoughts to Oliver's good points. The times when he was the most like his old self were always when he was rousing Peter. It was something that no one else could do, and though clearly just as hungry and impatient as the rest of them, Oliver seemed to relish the excitement of the situation, and also resented anyone who tried to help him. And when Peter did begin to respond, Oliver's spirits would soar. He would begin his part in the dance with a rhythm that none of the others possessed. And, unless the machine stopped at once and they got barely anything to eat, his high spirits would last, and he would be charming enough to keep them almost cheerful for several hours.

And cheerfulness, Abigail reflected, was certainly hard to come by in here. It was not only the constant, gnawing hunger, but the utter bleakness of this place that made it so unpleasant; the sensation of an endless succession of days without any comfort or diversion or interest.

But no, she said to herself, puzzled. *That isn't true anymore. There is something happening, or about to happen. Something very strange.* She sensed a chilling anticipation in the air around her, and shivered.

"When is Lola going to get back?" said Blossom. "I hate the way she goes away like this. The food machine could start any time. She's so selfish."

"But you've got to let her have some time to herself," said Abigail, trying to be good-natured in spite of the resentment she also felt.

"Why are you always defending her?" said Oliver. "She isn't perfect."

"She sure *isn't* perfect," said Blossom, hunched over the machine. "In fact, there's something I've been meaning to tell you about her. We're all stuck here together, I just think it's important to know what everybody is really like." Her face was pale and moist, and her eyes glittered as they shifted between Oliver and Abigail. "It was some things she said . . . about all of you."

Part of Abigail didn't want to hear, for she sensed that what Blossom was going to say would only make everything worse. Yet she was also curious, and Blossom's tone was too compelling to resist.

"Yes?" said Oliver, leaning forward eagerly. "What did she say?"

"Well," said Blossom. "It was really sinister and frightening. The first thing she said was about—"

"The dish ran away with the spoon," murmured hundreds of voices all around them, and Blossom's face was brilliantly colored, then suddenly white again, as the light began blinking on and off.

Abigail didn't bother to notice this time whether the light was red or green, for it really never made any difference. And also, she was preoccupied with other things, for as always, there was a time of frantic activity before the dance began.

"Wake him up!" Blossom shrieked, instantly in a frenzy, already beginning the movements of the dance. "Wake him up! Lolaaaa!" she screamed, her limbs twitching as she leaned over the edge. "Lola, get up here, the light's on!" She spun around to the others. "And don't tell her I was going to say anything!" she whispered vehemently. "Lolaaaa!" she screamed again, back at the edge. "Will you *get up here!*"

Oliver was shaking Peter's shoulders; Peter's head was lolling back and forth. "Come on, Peter!" Oliver cried, hopping nervously around him. "Come on, boy! We're gonna do our dance. Come on, Peter baby. We need you."

And then Lola was on the landing.

"At last!" Blossom shouted. "Where *were—*"

"Is he still out?" Lola said tensely, the muscles in her cheeks standing out as she stared at Peter. "For God's sake, wake him up!"

"That's what I'm *doing!*" Oliver screamed. "Leave me alone! Peter, please, Pete baby, it's Oliver talking to you, Oliver, your friend. I'm your friend, Pete, and I need you. Please Pete, come on."

Slowly Peter's eyes came into focus and he blinked at Oliver, then the others.

"Hurray! Good for you, Pete baby," Oliver cried. "Good for you!" And he pulled him affectionately to his feet.

"Oh, hurry!" Blossom wailed.

And they began.

Their dance was quite different now. Over the hungry days the patterns of their movements had been molded and shaped by the machine. They would always begin the dance just as they had done it the time before, and often they would be rewarded by a small pellet of food. But very often the second repetition had no effect. Watching each other closely, their movements would begin to change. Very slightly, one of them would move a little farther to the left or right, a hand would bend more at the wrist, a chin would lift, shoulders would sway. And if the change was the one the machine wanted, there would be another pellet of food, and the altered movement would continue and grow. Rhythm was important too: Once Oliver had moved his foot just before the next flash of the light instead of with it, and the syncopation of his movement had brought the reward.

At first it had been confusing and very difficult, for the possibilities of such subtle changes in movement were practically endless, and there was no way of knowing what the machine would prefer. It had been trial and error, and the errors had been numerous and heartbreaking. Too heartbreaking, in fact, to tolerate, for their hunger was intense. And it was just this intensity, the fact that they were operating under the direst necessity that any of them had ever known, that had created a new, specialized sense in each of them. It was a sense of what the machine would like, a feeling of its personality, so to speak. This, too, was a subtle thing, and none of them would have been able to explain it in words. Nevertheless they had all, sooner or later, unconsciously become aware of the pattern through which it was leading them; they had grown surer of their movements and how to change them, and from that point on the dance had steadily become more effective.

There were also those frustrating times when the voices would come and the light would flash, and yet nothing that they did would produce any food. But they had to dance on, no matter how long, for there was always the chance that food might come eventually, and that was a chance they could not afford to miss.

At this particular moment their dance went like this: Lola and Blossom, opposite one another, circled slowly around the hole in the landing. Their arms were extended above their heads, swaying from side to side, hands outstretched. As each one reached the point nearest the edge she would spin around quickly, timing it so that the spin occurred at every other flash of light; and at the moment of spinning, each would raise her head and emit a high-pitched wail. At the same time, Peter and Abigail, timing their movements precisely to the flashing light, performed a complex series of movements on two adjacent stairways —bowing to the landing, rising to their toes and waiting for a flash with their hands on their hips and their chins lifted, turning, lifting a leg behind and bending to touch a stair above with both hands, waiting for a flash, turning, moving quickly down to the landing to meet Oliver, waiting for a flash, then back up on the steps, where the pattern would begin again.

And Oliver. Oliver, in the center of it all, moved alone. He would begin between their two stairways, stretching, his back arched; then suddenly leap, landing on a flash of light and just missing Lola as she passed. Landing with one foot in the air and spinning around instantly to begin a swaying, hip-moving walk, his arms held before him, his hands and wrists twining and intertwining, his head bending toward one shoulder and then the other as he moved toward the stairs. There to meet, one every other time, Abigail or Peter. It was always Abigail the first time; he would reach her, grasp her about the waist, and with her body arched she would fall backwards, her hands brushing the floor, until at the right moment Oliver would pull her up to him, and he would step away to begin again. At the next repetition it would be Peter.

But now something was wrong. At the first repetition the pellet appeared, which was a relief, for it indicated that this was not one of those times when the dance was not going to work and they would have to go through it fruitlessly over and over again, hoping to be rewarded eventually. They began to relax during the second repetition, believing that the dance would be successful. But this time, no pellet appeared.

There was no need now for Lola to call out, as she had

done so often at the beginning, that it was time to change something. They all knew it without thinking, and intuitively they made the appropriate changes. And no pellet appeared.

Now they were getting anxious. It was like the beginning again, when they didn't know what changes to make. Their changes grew more extreme; and dreading the moment when the light would end, their eyes moved again and again to the slot on the floor.

And then, with only one small pellet lying on the landing, the light and the voices came to a sudden stop.

Blossom grabbed for it but Lola was closer and got there first. She held it above her head, scrambling up the steps out of the reach of the others. "Hold it!" she shouted as they pushed toward her. "Wait!"

"No!" Blossom squealed, stretching out her arm, but Lola popped the pellet into her mouth. Suddenly exhausted, Blossom sank back onto her step.

"But what happened?" asked Abigail, bewildered and afraid. "It hasn't done that for so long. We always seem to know how to change it now. . . ."

"We must have just not done it right," said Lola, swallowing guiltily. She sat down on a step. "Somebody made a mistake."

"No one made a mistake," said Oliver. "I was watching. Everybody was perfect. And the changes were right too. I could tell. It was trying to teach us something else, whenever it gives us food and then stops, it's trying to teach us something."

"Oh, why does it have to be so complicated?" said Blossom.

Oliver was still thinking. "Wait a minute . . . ," he said. "It was trying to teach us something . . . we did the dance right, and we made the right changes . . . but it still wasn't satisfied, because . . . because it was trying to teach us to do something else, something that wasn't the dance at all."

"Yes," said Abigail slowly. "Actually, that kind of makes sense."

Oliver was beginning to get excited. For the first time, something he had suggested seemed to make more sense than what Lola said. "When we first got here, we never would have thought the food machine could make us do anything as complicated as that dance," he said. "It would have seemed impossible. But it wasn't impossible, we did learn the dance. And now that we've learned it, and we don't make any mistakes, it's trying to teach us to do something else, to do something else when the light *isn't* flashing!"

"Okay, okay," Lola said. "Maybe you're right. But remember how long it took us to learn the dance? How will we ever learn what this new thing is?"

Oliver was sitting very erectly, his face glowing from exertion. "We'll learn it, I know we will," he said. *He was like his old self again,* thought Abigail. "I think it's really exciting," he went on. "Something new is going to start happening now. We'll just figure out what it wants us to do, and do it, and then when the light comes on and we dance, then we'll know if we did the right thing."

"But that's so complicated," Blossom whined. "And what if we don't figure it out, then we'll just have to keep waiting longer and longer and I can't stand it why did Lola get the food I'm so—"

"Oh, cut it out," Lola sighed. "I'll give you one of mine next time."

"But when is next time going to be? What if he's right,

that it wants us to do something else? How will we ever know what it is?" Blossom moaned. "Why did you get the food, why are you so selfish? I'm so hungry!"

Lola put her hands over her ears and shook her head back and forth. "Oh, shut up! Shut up!" she cried, and jumped to her feet. "Everyone else is just as hungry as you! Why do you think *you're* the only one who feels it? And I can't stand your horrible squeaky voice!" She turned and dashed up the stairs.

For a long moment Blossom stared after her, her lips quivering, as a bright spot of color appeared on each sallow cheek. She narrowed her eyes and turned to the others. "I've been saving this up for a long time, maybe too long," she said. Her voice was crisp, but shaking slightly.

"The thing you were going to tell us, about Lola?" Oliver asked in an excited whisper.

Blossom nodded. "Only it wasn't one thing, it was more than that. It was what she said about everybody. Including you!" she added suddenly, turning to Peter. "You never want to say anything against her, but you know what she said? I'm just telling you for your own good. She said it was real depressing at first, when she thought you were the only other person here, because you were such a 'helpless simp—' "

But why is she doing this? Abigail wondered, watching Peter apprehensively to see the effect of Blossom's story. As usual, his face had no expression, but he seemed to slump down a little more with each vindictive word.

"—and all you'd do was slow her down. Isn't that disgusting? You'd think she would have wanted to help you, but all she thought about was herself."

"But," Peter protested feebly, his eyes moist, "but she—"

"I don't care what she did, or what she said to you. All I know is what she said to me." She turned to Oliver. "And you!" she went on with hardly a pause. "What she said about you! How even though you never knew what was really going on, you still pretended to be this 'big, tough-guy leader,' " she mimicked Lola's sarcastic voice. "And how you made her think of a girl when you were singing the first time she saw you—"

Abigail felt her face flush. What Blossom was doing was incomprehensible to her—telling people mean things that someone had said about them. Talking behind someone's back was different, of course, everyone did that, and as long as the person in question didn't find out there was nothing wrong with it. But to actually *tell* people these things! It was like a nightmare.

"Like a girl!" Blossom spat out the words with relish. "And that she typed you as a phony from beginning to end. She said you were only pretending to be brave, but were really scared to death, and that the only reason you could act tough was that there was only Peter and some girls around, you were just trying to impress Abigail, and if a *real* guy had been here he would have had you under his thumb in a minute. And you," she continued, turning to Abigail, leaving Oliver shaking with rage behind her. "And you, why she said she was sure that you would fall for Oliver, that you were too dumb to see through his phony games, that you were spineless enough to let him use you and do anything he wanted with you—"

Abigail was shaking her head miserably. It was hard to believe that Lola would have said that to Blossom; but again, Abigail found herself believing every word, every word like a knife twisting inside her. Blossom was so definite, so convincing, so *reasonable* in some absurd way that it was impossible to discard what she said. As the first tears began trickling down her cheeks, Abigail felt an unthinking rage against Lola growing inside her.

"That you acted so sweet and nice to everybody, so simpering, and then you would just let Oliver walk all over you because you were so spineless that you were hardly a person at all, just this blonde, empty-headed *thing* who only cared what other people thought about her—"

Blossom stopped suddenly and took a deep breath. "*Now* do you see what I mean about her? I'm just telling you this for your own good, so you'll know what she's really like."

"She. . . ." Oliver, his face red, seemed to be having trouble getting the words out. "She seems to think . . . that bitch seems to think she knows more about us than we do. If she was a boy I'd beat the piss out of her!"

"But how could she *say* that?" Abigail was weeping openly now, her hands over her eyes, not only miserable, but furious as well. "How could she *say* things like that?"

There were quick footsteps above them. "Shhh!" said Blossom. "Here she comes."

Abigail hastily wiped her eyes and pushed her hair back out of her face. She didn't want Lola to know she had been crying, and turned her head away as Lola stepped lightly down to the landing.

Lola didn't seem to notice that anything was wrong. "Look," she said to Blossom in her ordinary voice, "I'm sorry I yelled at you. I know that kind of thing bothers you, but you know what I'm like, how I talk. It doesn't mean anything."

Blossom was smirking slightly. "Yes, I know," she said. "It doesn't matter."

"I was just worried about the machine not working, that's all." Lola sat down on her stairway. "Anyway, I've been thinking about what you said," she said to Oliver. "And I guess it does make sense. It's the only explanation. The machine was trying to teach us something by offering the food first, but this time changing the dance wasn't what it wanted us to do. It wants us to do something else, like you said."

"Mmm," said Oliver, avoiding her eyes.

"Well?" Lola said. "Hey, what's with you guys, anyway?"

No one answered her.

"Did I say something wrong, or something?"

"Oh, no, no," Blossom said lightly, folding her hands in her lap and pursing her lips.

"Yeah, well look, we've got a lot of thinking to do. It's not gonna be easy figuring out what this damn thing wants us to do now but—" She stopped suddenly, leaning forward in her seat and looking around at all of them. "Hey, come on now, something's up. Peter, what's going on here? Why won't anybody look at me?"

Peter slumped in his seat, looking down. "Nothing . . . it's. . . ."

"What were you guys talking about just now, anyway?"

"Oh, nothing really," Blossom said. "Just chatting."

"Yeah," Lola said. "Well, big deal. Whatever the hell is wrong with you, we've got something really important to think about now, and pretty soon you'll all be hungry enough to go along with me. Now, what I think we should do is—"

"Well, maybe we just don't *care* what you think we should do, you smart-ass bitch," said Oliver, his voice rich with contempt.

"Huh?" Lola said, squinting at him, too stunned by his sudden outburst to know how to respond.

"He's just tired of you thinking you're better than anyone else, and always bossing us around," Blossom said sweetly. "Just like we all are."

"Hey, now wait a minute," Lola said slowly. "Who's bossing everybody around? All I was—"

"Yes!" said Oliver. "Tired of you and your whole stinking attitude. Tired of your lousy pronouncements, tired of what you think we are and the dumb, stupid things you say about us!"

"Oho," said Lola, standing and stepping down to the landing, her fists clenched. "Oho, now I think I'm beginning to understand."

"Good!" Oliver shouted, and Abigail began to sob miserably. "I've sat here listening to you pretend you're the leader long enough. Now we can see through you, you lousy bitch, and we're all sick of you. Do you understand?"

"Yes, I do understand!" Lola said, moving threateningly toward Blossom. "You were telling them things about me, weren't you? Telling them everything I said, and probably a lot more besides. No wonder you were so fawning and sweetsie that day, why you ripped that dumb skirt; so you could get me to talk, and then distort it and tell the others. And you're crazy; it's insane, it's completely insane!" She shook her open hand at her. "Don't you realize what you're doing? Don't you know that you're hurting *them* just as much as me? You're just *using* them to get back at

me! You're going to ruin everything! It's inhuman!" Suddenly her voice dropped and she took a step closer, shaking her head back and forth. "You don't give a shit about another living thing, do you? All you care about is your own fat self, and so you go around in this inhuman way *betraying* people, you—"

"The dish ran away with the spoon," said the voices to Abigail, and in an instant they were all on their feet, dancing frantically.

At the first repetition there was a whir and a click and a pellet on the floor. Changing nothing, filled with fear and hope, they repeated the dance exactly. And there was another pellet, followed by a general gasp of confusion and surprise.

And as she danced, and the pellets kept coming, Abigail tried to understand what had made it work. She remembered the premonition she had felt just a short while before, the chilling premonition, and for a moment she wondered if the answer lay there. But suddenly she was afraid to think about it. She wanted to lose herself in the dance, to dance and dance; and then to eat, and forget.

chapter **13**

"But what did we do that made it work?" said Blossom.

Oliver had no idea what the answer was. He was still furious at Lola. He felt stubborn and ornery, and wanted to make Blossom's question seem trivial and unimportant. "It just decided to work again, that's all," he said, shrugging.

"No, that can't be it," said Lola, chewing on her nail. "There's got to be a reason for it. This goddam thing has a reason for everything."

"You . . . you're right," Abigail said hesitantly. "It always does."

"Oh, why do you always think she's right?" Oliver snapped at her. "Didn't you hear what Blossom told us about her? Why do you pay any attention to the dumb bitch?"

"But . . . ," said Abigail, who seemed to be about to cry, "but I . . . I mean she . . . just because. . . ."

"Oh, stop whimpering!" cried Oliver, suddenly in a

rage. "I'm sick of your stupid whimpering!" And he grabbed Abigail by the hair and shook her head roughly back and forth.

"Nude in the house of be careful in Oliver's food will be coming she gobbled him up in the dish ran away with the," said the voices to all of them. And the light was flashing again, flashing brightly not five minutes after it had stopped; and they were dancing.

"But why?" Abigail said aloud through her tears, unable to keep from asking, even though the terrible answer was there, inside her, someplace where she didn't want to look. She bent forward, touched the step with her hands, lifted her leg in the air, turned around, down to the landing, to feel Oliver's hands around her waist, bending backward, then rising. "What made it work?" Back to the steps. "Was it because we were fighting?" Bowing to the landing, rising to her toes. "Does it want us to *fight*?"

Lola spun around and wailed. "No," she called out hoarsely, dancing around the hole. "Oh my God. I think . . . it wasn't just fighting." She spun around and wailed. "We've had fights before. It was more than that. Oh my God, it must be. . . ." She spun around and wailed. "It was Blossom, ratting on me, betraying me. And then Oliver, hurting you because of it. *That's* what it wants us to do!"

With slow regularity the pellets rolled out one by one onto the landing.

chapter **14**

Lola backed away and sat down rather shakily on her step, swallowing her last morsel of food. They had been particularly well fed, and for the first time in many days, though she certainly could have eaten more, the hunger was no longer a gnawing pain. It had, however, been replaced by something worse.

Up until this moment, she had been able to put up with being here fairly well, she thought. After the initial pain of withdrawal, for example, she had begun to actually be glad she wasn't smoking, for she felt so much better without it. And then she had begun the discipline of running, which not only helped to alleviate the terrible boredom of this place, but also increased her feeling of physical well-being. She hated being here, of course, but she was just beginning to feel that she might be able to tolerate it.

But now something else was happening, and the thought of it suddenly caused her shoulders to twitch in an involuntary spasm of apprehension. The stairways around her—they were no longer simply bleak and sterile and cold, they had begun to take on an actual personality that hung menacingly in the air around them. They almost seemed to *look* different now, and suddenly their appearance was terrifying to her.

Abigail cleared her throat, turning toward Lola. "What you said when we were dancing," she began. "You know about how Blossom . . . telling what you said about us, and Oliver, pulling my hair, how that made it work. . . ?"

"Yeah?" Lola said, feeling her heart pound heavily.

"Well . . . well, that seems so crazy." Abigail leaned forward urgently. "Why should it want us to do that?"

"Why should it want us to do all the other crazy things it makes us do?"

"But . . . but that's so horrible. How can it want us to do horrible things like that?"

"Horrible?" Oliver asked, raising his eyebrows. "All she was doing was telling us the truth. I think it makes sense. The machine is trying to get us to always tell the truth."

"What?" said Blossom, startled. "Always tell the—"

Lola interrupted her. "Yes, that's all very sweet and nice, but what makes you so sure that what she was saying *was* the truth?"

"Because it all made sense," Oliver said complacently. "They were just the kind of things you *would* say about us, that's why. And why should she make it up, anyway?"

"Yes," Blossom said haughtily. "Why should I make anything up about *you?*"

"I can think of plenty of reasons," said Lola, and sighed with a kind of hopeless fatigue. Peter was looking at her with wide eyes, and she gestured at him, her arm swinging down loosely. "You might as well go back to sleep, Pete, or whatever it is you do. It's gonna get pretty messy in here now."

"I don't know what she's talking about," said Blossom quickly. "Just because the machine happened to start working again at that particular time she seems to think it means something."

Lola stood up. "Oh, I don't even care what you say. Go on talking. It won't make any difference to you, because you do what it wants anyway."

She left them and wandered, brooding miserably. She tried to convince herself that it really *was* a coincidence that the machine had starting working again when it had, but she was unable to. It all fit together so well: doing the dance correctly, the machine indicating it was willing to feed them but not doing so; and then Blossom telling those rotten secrets she had been saving for so long, and Oliver hurting Abigail, and the machine suddenly, immediately responding both times. Even if the evidence was only circumstantial, Lola was convinced that the machine's intention was to turn them all against one another. It just seemed right; it was exactly the kind of thing this cruel place would want to do to them.

And what kind of things would they begin to do now; now that they were going to be starved into becoming one another's deadly enemies? Lola considered this question, feeling the short hairs on her neck begin to rise. Blossom would just go on doing what she had always done anyway, of course, but what would someone like Oliver do, or Abigail? Lola shook her head, unable to think. Food was the most important thing here, and she knew that if they were hungry enough, there was nothing they wouldn't do to get it.

And suddenly she sank down on the step, overcome, and felt the tears begin pouring down her face, felt her body, thinner than ever now, convulsed by deep sobs. Now she was really helpless, there was nothing she could do against this thing that was happening; and she was utterly alone, for the rest of them wouldn't even *admit* what was happening, let alone go along with her and fight it. They would follow the machine like unthinking robots; and, in the end, so would she.

That was when she noticed the footsteps. She jumped to her feet. Far below her a figure with pale short hair was moving resolutely up the stairs.

chapter 15

He had known she would be surprised. The thought of her reaction, in fact, had been part of what had driven him to push himself to his feet and march away from them. "I . . . I have to go to the toilet," he had explained when they gaped up at him, hardly believing their eyes.

But why had Oliver seemed so displeased? "Don't you want me to help you, like I usually do?" he had asked him, starting to get up.

"No," Peter had said quickly, and hurried away.

"For Christ sake," Lola said, as he reached her in the middle of a flight. "What are you doing, walking around by yourself?"

"Please, could . . . could we try to find a landing? I . . . I feel funny here."

"Sure, sure," said Lola, eyeing him rather suspiciously. "Sure, kid, anything you say."

There was a landing not too far away. He sank down against an ascending flight, feeling all at once the sweat of his ordeal. Lola stood watching him, her eyes half closed.

He had no idea how to begin. He hadn't really thought about what he was going to say, he only knew what he felt; and now, when he was faced with it, his mind was suddenly a blank. And what finally did come out, when Lola began to seem impatient, was no careful preparation for what he wanted to tell her; it was the blunt, basic fact at the center of his thoughts. "You . . . you're not going to . . . to go along with it, are you?"

"What?" she said, her eyes widening as she leaned toward him. "What are you talking about?"

"But . . . but don't you know?" Her reaction wasn't nearly as satisfying as he had expected; he was probably messing it all up. With an effort, he began again. "I don't care what Blossom says. The machine. What you said about . . . about what it wants us to do now. I . . . I just felt you . . . you wouldn't go along with it, like . . . like they will." And suddenly he felt such an urgency that the words, for him, practically tumbled out. "And, and they *will* go along with it, I know they will, and . . . and then I was more afraid than before, but it was different . . . it was different because I thought of you . . . of, of . . . of you, and what you're like and how you would *never* . . . and I just wanted to tell you, to tell you . . . I want to, to try it too. Maybe if . . . if *both* of us won't do it, then, then maybe the others won't, or something. I don't know. Please, can we try it, I . . . I'm never that hungry anyway." He looked down into his lap, afraid to see her face.

In the silence that followed a hundred terrible thoughts raced through his mind. She would laugh at him, she would think he was being ridiculous; he was wrong about her, she wanted to go along with the machine, she was up here plotting against them, against *him* in particular; remember what Blossom said, how Lola thought he was this pitiful weakling, she wouldn't believe him, she wouldn't trust him, she would laugh at him—

His thoughts were interrupted, not by a sound, but by a touch. He looked up. Lola was kneeling beside him, her hand on his shoulder; and most amazing of all, her eyes were filled with tears. "Peter," she said, her voice rough (Lola crying? But how could that be?), "Peter, do you think we can? Do you really think we can do it?"

"But . . . but don't you want to? Yes, I think . . . I think we can do it, if you want to."

"And if *you* want to," she said, gripping his shoulder tightly. "Not alone, though. Even I," and she smiled through her tears, an open kind of smile he had never seen on her before. "Even *I* probably couldn't do it by myself. I need you, if it's going to work. You are *essential*. Do you understand that?"

"I . . . I guess so," he said, confused. He hadn't expected this at all. First, the shock of her tears, and now her admitting that she couldn't do it on her own. He had expected her to be supremely self-confident, as usual; to accept his offer of help as an insignificant, perhaps mildly useful (though certainly not necessary!) gesture. But suddenly she actually seemed to be depending on him to help her. That was the biggest shock of all, and it was not a pleasant one. The responsibility was frightening, and heavy to bear. No one had ever depended on him; he had never been strong enough or good enough at anything for that. It was he who depended on others, on Oliver, on Jasper. Jasper, who had always taken care of him. Jasper. . . .

"Hey!" Her voice was hard and sharp again. "Peter! Snap out of it!"

"Huh?" He blinked at her.

There were no tears in her eyes now, and her mouth was set in a firm line. "Now listen to me, Peter. Listen carefully." Her hand was still gripping his shoulder, and as she spoke she shook it from time to time for emphasis. "This thing we're going to do is going to be hard, real hard. But just remember, *you* came to me with it. I'm not forcing you into anything. Do you understand that?"

He nodded.

"Okay. Remember it, then." She looked away for a moment, biting her lip, as if she were gathering her thoughts. Then she began again. "And also remember this: This thing we're fighting, this place, the people who are doing it, whatever the hell it is, it's tricky, it's real tricky. And it's in control. Everything is on its side. They have all the machines in the world and they've got us trapped, and they can do whatever they want to us. And we don't have anything. We have nothing to fight it with except ourselves, our own bodies and our brains. And they're going to take advantage of any slips we make. So *we can't slip.* Do you understand that?"

He nodded again.

"And you know what I mean, don't you? You can't go off into these . . . daydreams, or, or trances, or whatever they are. They will use that against us, I don't know how, but in some way they will. You've got to keep alert. You've got to keep alert or it will all fall apart. Peter! Did you hear me? These trances have got to stop!"

"But . . . ," he said, "but. . . ." What was she saying? How could he stop them? They were the only good thing there was, the only comfort he had from the terrifying heights and the bleakness and Oliver's sporadic cruelty and equally sporadic interest. And anyway, they were beyond his control, they were like a fog coming and blotting everything out, there was nothing he could do about them because he wasn't creating them; something else was. "But . . . but I can't," he said. "I . . . I can't help it, they just happen to me."

"Well, you've got to help it." She was squeezing his shoulder very tightly now, her bitten-off fingernails pressing painfully against the bone. "You have got to help it. If you can't stop them, we're lost. And don't give me that bullshit about something else doing it. It's nothing but yourself, you're just doing it to yourself."

"I . . . I am?"

"Oh, of *course* you are!" She let go of his shoulder to gesture into the air and then, dropping her voice, she asked, "What are they like, anyway?"

"I. . . ." It was difficult to describe, and so embarrassing. But, watching her face, he knew he had to try. If he didn't at least tell her about them, then his whole difficult journey, alone, step by painful step up to her, would have been useless. "Well, it's. . . ." He sighed. "Once, when we were first here, I think . . . I think I told you about . . . about the first orphanage I was in, the good one . . . ?"

"Yes?" She nodded her encouragement, and her face was serious and concerned.

"I . . . it's like I'm back there again, except it's different, better, kind of . . . well, kind of magical. And there's . . . well, this boy. . . ." His voice was barely a whisper now; he had never spoken about Jasper to anyone. "This boy . . . he was my friend, he . . . we were always together. Jasper, his name was Jasper. He looked kind of like . . . like Oliver. And he's in the dream, in the . . . in the magic room, taking care of me. . . ." Now he was beginning to cry, his throat constricting and tears welling up in his eyes. "Taking care of me . . . he always took care of me . . . taking care of me and, and . . . and loving me." He gasped back a sob and covered his eyes with his hand.

Lola said nothing, and at last he took his hand away and looked at her. She was still studying him intently, but her face had softened. "It was the best time in your life," she murmured.

"Yes."

"And now is the worst, and you want to go back to that other time."

"I . . . is that it, do you think?"

"It sure seems like it. And . . . and in a certain way I can understand it. You've been dumped on ever since that first place, but something always kept you going anyway, until you got in here; and then in here, everything was so awful that you just gave up, and tried to get back there. Doesn't that make sense?"

"Yes . . . yes, I guess it does."

"And I know it feels good to go back there," she went on, "but listen: There's something else that would feel even better. Beating this place, winning out against it, wouldn't that be great, Peter, knowing that you'd done that?" She was leaning forward, her eyes pleading, her hand on his shoulder again. "And if we don't, if we don't win . . . Christ, the only alternative is what that damn machine is going to make us do to each other. You know that, that's why you came all the way up here by yourself to find me."

"Yes." He was nodding at her. "Yes, I know what it would do. Yes, it would be terrible."

"And going back to your dream world won't help at

all. You've got to realize that if we can only win out, right *now* can be better than the dream. Do you think you can, Peter?"

"Oh, I don't know!" Suddenly his voice was raised in agony, his fists clenched. "How can I make it stop?"

"Okay, okay." She seemed taken aback by his outburst. "Maybe not all at once, maybe you have to go back sometimes, but remember what I said. Will you do that? It's our only hope."

"I'll remember." He took a deep breath. He was staring straight into her eyes. Strangely enough, what he had told her about Jasper made it possible for him to look at her directly, as he had never looked at her before. "But how . . . how *can* we fight the machine? What can we do?"

Lola sighed and stood up, taking a few quick paces back and forth across the small landing. "Oh, God," she murmured under her breath, as though he weren't there. "Oh, God, it's gonna be tough, it's gonna be so goddam tough." Suddenly she spun toward him, pointing. "Because we're gonna be fighting two things. The machine isn't the only enemy. It's the others, too, we're gonna have to be fighting the others too."

"Are . . . are you sure?"

"You said so yourself. You said they'd go along with it, and you're right, God damn it! If only there was just *one* of them who'd side with us, then at least it would be three against two. I wonder if maybe Abigail. . . . But no." She sighed. "Anyway, there's only one thing we can do about it. The first thing we've got to do is tell them what we're doing, and even *beg* them to be on our side." She was staring intensely off into the distance, clasping her hands so tightly together that he could see the muscles standing out on her thin arms.

"But . . . but if you don't think Abigail would go along with us, maybe . . . well, maybe we could get Oliver . . . ?"

"What? *Oliver?* Are you kidding?" She dropped her arms and snorted contemptuously. "Oliver? You know, Pete, in some ways you're pretty smart, I'm beginning to realize that. But in other ways you're mighty dumb. Oliver? Do you think for one minute he'd even—" Then she noticed his face, and stopped herself. "Listen, Peter," she went on more carefully. "I know you have this thing about Oliver, and now I can even understand it a little. I know he's like that friend you want to go back to, but you can't trust him." Suddenly she broke off, her eyes hardening. "You don't believe me, do you? You think I just don't like him, like Blossom said."

"No . . . I . . . maybe you're right about him, but. . . ."

"Listen to this, Peter. Listen." She spoke slowly and distinctly. "He *likes* those trances of yours, because he's the only one who can wake you up. He *likes* you to be helpless, so he can be stronger. Don't you see that? He's using you."

"But . . . ," said Peter. He was going to cry again. It was too much to take, Lola telling him he had to fight against the magic room, and now losing whatever small comfort he got occasionally from Oliver.

"Peter, please, listen to me." She was pleading with him again. "I'm sorry I had to tell you that, it was a Blossom kind of trick, and I'm sorry. And the machine will probably like it that I told you. But if you trust him it will only weaken you." She was grasping both his shoulders now, shaking him again. "You *can* stand on your own. I'll help you. I know it's not the same, but I'll help you."

"Okay, okay." He shook the tears out of his eyes and

109

turned his face away from her. She had said enough; now he had to think it through by himself.

"But about the machine," he said, clearing his throat. "What can we do about that?"

"Oh yeah." She stood up and stepped away from him. "The machine. I guess there's only one thing we can do. You know what it is as well as I do. You already said it; I've been trying not to. You know what it is, don't you?"

He nodded.

"We just can't do what it wants, and can't go along with the others when they do. Which means that most of the time . . . most of the time we won't, we won't. . . ."

He finished for her. "We won't be able to eat."

chapter 16

"Maybe he's up there talking to Lola," Blossom said. Peter had been gone much longer than it should have taken him to go to the toilet. Blossom was nervous whenever anyone was away from the machine for more than a few minutes. She herself left the landing as little as possible, and was always trying to make the others stay around: The thought of losing out when the machine might be generous was unbearable to her.

"Why would he be talking to Lola?" said Oliver, sounding strangely tense. "What would he have to say to her?"

"I don't know." Twisting her hair, Blossom studied the stairways above her yet another time. "But they better get back here pretty soon, that's all I can say."

Abigail had moved from the stairway she usually shared with Oliver and had been sitting by herself, staring into her lap. "But if Lola was right, then it doesn't matter," she said slowly. "The machine won't give us anything to eat until somebody does something against somebody else;

so we can just wait till they come back to do it." There was an unusual bitterness in her voice.

"You mean you *believed* that crap?" said Oliver. "God, you must be even stupider than I thought you were. She was just hysterical because we'd all found out what she said about us. She didn't know what she was talking about. The whole thing was a coincidence. It had nothing to do with what Blossom or I did."

Blossom didn't agree with him, but she said nothing. She wasn't yet absolutely sure that Lola was right, but she certainly hoped she was. Whatever might happen, Blossom knew that she was the most experienced at doing what Lola claimed the machine wanted, and would therefore be better off than the others. She was eager for an opportunity to test Lola's theory, and began trying to think what she might do as an experiment. It was not long before an idea came to her.

"I bet Peter *is* talking to Lola," she said. "I bet they're planning something."

"What the hell is *that* supposed to mean?" said Oliver, and Abigail looked up from her lap.

"Oh, I don't know," said Blossom, looking away coyly and letting her finger play with her lip. "I mean, of course Lola's idea that the machine wants us to gang up against each other is utterly infantile and stupid, but *she* believes it, doesn't she? And that probably means she's going to try something, doesn't it, to make the machine work? Something against us. And you know what Peter's like, anybody can make him do anything. I'm sure that's what they're doing."

"Oh, come on now," Abigail pleaded. "You can't keep saying things like that. It's not reasonable. Don't you remember how Lola acted when she said it? She hated the whole idea! She's not going to go and start doing it right away."

"How come you're always defending her?" Oliver asked Abigail suspiciously. "You know what she's really like. Why do you have to keep questioning it?"

"But Oliver. I don't understand. You keep contradicting yourself. I mean, it was practically your whole idea that the machine wants us to do something else now. But just a minute ago you said it was only a coincidence."

"So what? I can say whatever I want. I don't have to account to you for what I say. And I think Blossom's right about her, too."

"Listen," Blossom said. "I hear footsteps. They're coming back." And now, for the first time, Blossom herself felt curious about what Peter and Lola had been up to, rather than just irritated. Obviously they had been together, for they arrived on the landing at the same time: Lola first, loose-limbed and self-conscious, and Peter, rather hunched, behind her.

"Uh, listen," Lola said, after a moment, when no one had greeted her. "Uh, Peter and I . . . we've been talking about some things, and—"

"Yes, we figured you must have been," said Oliver venomously. "We figured you were probably up there planning and—"

"Please," Lola said. "Please, this one time, try to forget all that crap and believe me. Please believe me, this is too important to mess up." She was twisting her hands together and there was a hoarse earnestness in her voice. "Listen, this machine, it's . . . whether you admit it or not, you *know* what it's doing now; it's trying to turn us all against each other. And listen, I was thinking up there, there's probably *people* behind the machine, and they must be watching us, or else they wouldn't know when to turn it on and off. And we can't let them control us like this, and make us do terrible things. If we go along with them now, there's no telling *what* they will make us do next." She looked from one of them to another. There was no response. She took a deep breath. "So Peter and I . . . we decided we're not going to go along with it. It was his idea as much as mine. And if we all stand against the machine together, then they'll see they can't control us. They'll give up, and we'll be the winners. But if anybody, even one person, stays with them, and goes along with the machine, then they'll probably keep trying and trying to get us all, and we won't have much of a chance. So, please fight it with us." She sighed, lifting her hands; and then, tilting her head to the side and biting her thumbnail, she waited.

"But how?" Abigail said. "How can we fight it? What can we possibly do?"

"Well," Lola said, with an uncomfortable little cough. "That's the hard part, of course." She paused for a moment. "All we can do is just refuse to do what it wants, just *refuse* to do it. And of course, that means for a while we won't get much to eat, I guess, but—"

That was all Blossom needed. Not be able to eat? How intolerable! She had to stop the idea; to do something that would put herself in control again. And she found it quite easily. She began to giggle.

Lola stopped in the middle of her sentence and spun toward her, blushing; Abigail, Oliver, and even Peter stared at her in surprise.

"Oh, I'm sorry!" Blossom gasped, letting her giggle expand into laughter. "Oh!" She swayed back and forth, wiping her eyes. "Oh, my!" She hiccuped, put one still-plump hand over her mouth, and let her eyes slide from side to side. "I'm sorry," she said at last, finally getting her laughter under control, "but I just couldn't help it. The way she's trying to sound so brave and self-sacrificing, and yet what she's really doing is so obvious. And she thinks we're going to fall for it, that's the funniest part. Oh! And her hair all sticking up like that, and her trying to seem like a heroine, with that hair! It's too much."

She had never seen Lola look so defeated. Lola reached up and touched her hair with one hand, then walked to her stairway and sat down without a word, giving Peter a meaningful glance. Blossom didn't like that glance.

But Abigail was talking to Blossom now. "What do you mean? I don't know what you're talking about." She seemed terribly confused and upset; and Oliver was obviously trying to keep his feelings under control. "What do you mean, 'What she's really doing'? Why don't you believe her?"

"Because I just don't," said Blossom. She was furious now. Lola's glance couldn't have said more plainly that she had expected Blossom to respond this way all along. It was a conspiracy between Lola and Peter against her. "Didn't you hear what she just said? She thinks the machine wants us to hurt each other, and that's what she's trying to do. She's trying to trick us, so she can prove how stupid and gullible we are. And then laugh at us, make us starve ourselves because she says so, and then laugh. Don't you see?" Blossom's voice grew shrill with urgency. Both of them, even Oliver, who was usually on her side, looked doubtful. They must have believed Lola! And now Lola had Peter; she couldn't let her get Oliver and Abigail too. She reached for the only weapon she had. "Don't you remember what I told you about her? How she said Abigail was a simpering, empty-headed thing, and how Oliver was only pretending to be brave to show off but really—"

"Yes, yes, I remember," Oliver interrupted quickly. "I remember enough not to pay any attention to anything she says. What the hell do you think you're going to do, anyway?" he asked Lola belligerently. "Not do the dance anymore?"

"That . . . that was the general idea," she said rather stiffly.

Oliver snorted. "Sure you are! I'd like to see you *try* not to dance when that light comes on."

At that moment it dawned on Blossom what Lola really meant, and what she could do; and the terrifying consequences and sudden emergency of the situation threatened to send her into total hysteria. For, even deserted by them all, Lola still had the power not to dance, and keep them from eating. Blossom had to prevent it. But at the moment she didn't know how, and tried not to let the fear show in her voice. "And Peter won't be able to keep from dancing either," she said. "He's too weak to do anything."

"Yes, I know," Oliver said, staring at Peter without expression.

"But Oliver!" Peter cried out.

And then Lola was on her feet. "You know something?" she said to Blossom. "You are really amazing. A phenomenon. Do you realize they were about to go along with it? And you ruined it, you ruined all our chances of getting through this thing without being—"

"Without being what?" Blossom demanded. "You don't even know what you're talking about. You *say* you won't dance, but you will." Lola had to be weakened, she had to be convinced that nothing she did would make any difference. It was the only thing Blossom could think of doing. "You might as well give up right now. Even if you could keep from dancing, your little plan would never work because *I* won't let it. Do you understand? No matter what you do, I'm going to ruin it, I'm going to ruin *everything* you try!"

At that moment the light and the voices began, and before they knew it they were all dancing. And Lola and Peter were dancing too.

Blossom felt a surge of happiness and relief as the pellets began rolling out. Lola, for all her big words, wasn't going to interfere after all! Blossom couldn't control herself. "See?" she crowed with delight. "See? Lola and her big mouth is dancing too."

"No!" came a strangled cry from the stairway. "Don't, Lola! Stop! We've—" Peter came lurching toward her. The food stopped.

Lola blinked, and stood still, as Peter grabbed her. "Peter!" she said. "I—"

"Stop it! Stop it!" Blossom shrieked in terror. "What are you doing? Dance, dance, you've got to keep—"

Lola turned on her, her face alive with anger and determination. "No! No! No!" she shouted, and she put her hands over her ears. "Peter, hold your ears! Don't look at that light! Come on, up the stairs, follow me!"

"No!" Blossom wailed, grabbing Lola's shoulder and trying to pull her back into the dance. "You can't do this!"

"Oh yes we can!" cried Lola, and shoved Blossom to the other side of the landing. She grabbed Peter's arm, the

117

other hand still over her ear, and began leading him, stumbling, up the stairs, away from the light. They moved in slow motion, with tremendous effort, as though fighting a powerful current. But the higher they got, the faster they began to climb, until at last they disappeared in the tangle of stairways above.

"Food will be coming soon," the voices murmured dully to Blossom as she danced helplessly, beginning to sob. "Food will be coming soon. Food will be coming soon. Food. . . ."

chapter 17

Abigail was the first to come.

When they caught sight of her, far below, they both hoped for a moment that she might be joining them. But as she approached they could tell, from something abject in the way she was trudging up the steps, that she was not coming over to their side. And they were right.

"Please come back," she said, practically wringing her hands. Her face was very pale, except for the darkness underneath her eyes. "Please, we're all so hungry."

"We're hungry too," Lola said.

"Oh, and it's so awful down there! Both of them, they're . . . when they're hungry they can be so. . . ."

"They're taking it all out on you, aren't they?" Lola asked her. "And they made you come up here and beg because they knew you were the only one I'd pay any attention to, right?"

Abigail nodded mutely.

Lola sighed. "Listen, Abigail, why not just forget about

them and stay up here with us? You won't be any hungrier up here than you are down there, and we'll be decent to you."

"But if I didn't go back, Oliver would be so angry. He'd hate me, he really would hate me."

"So? So what if that bastard hates you? You know he's not worth it."

"But . . . but maybe she'd rather be with him anyway," Peter said softly, looking away.

"Oh, I don't know, I don't know," Abigail moaned, twisting her hands. "But now . . . now I have to go back. Are you *sure* you won't come with me? Don't you want to eat?"

"Don't you want to beat the machine?" Lola said.

Oliver came next. His walk was both belligerent and apprehensive, like a man swaggering to the gallows. He spoke to Peter, his eyes flickering only occasionally over to Lola, who regarded him silently, squatting with hunched shoulders, her mouth in a hard line.

"Come on, Pete," Oliver began, in the cajoling tones he had once used to wake him from his dreams. "*I* know what you're trying to do; *I* understand. Okay, you've proven that you can be strong and . . . do things on your own. But don't you remember how much fun it was when we did things together?"

Lola fought her desire to stop him, trying to appear indifferent but really watching Peter nervously. And Peter, hearing that warm, familiar voice so close to him, the voice that had been the only thing comforting enough to bring him back from his other world, felt his breath catch in his throat and his resolution begin to give way. He looked down, avoiding Oliver's eyes, feeling the terrifying vast spaces pressing down on him, feeling the gnawing hunger and his loneliness, thinking of Jasper–Oliver. And it would be so easy to make everything comfortable again. All he had to do was stand up and let Oliver lead him back; back to depending on Oliver for everything, back to his magic room. And if he went, Lola would come too, and they could eat. She had said he was essential, she had said she couldn't do it on her own.

"Come on, Pete. What do you think you're doing up here anyway? Starving ourselves won't make things any better. Don't you know that?"

But strangely enough, it was the fact that he was essential that kept Peter from giving in. When Lola had first said she needed him it had been terrifying; but now he couldn't bear to think of what would happen, and how she would feel, if he deserted her. Still unable to look at Oliver directly, he said, in a near whisper, "No, Oliver, I . . . I think it would be better if I stayed here."

"But, but Peter," Oliver said brokenly, as though something very precious was being torn away from him, "Peter, we *need* you down there."

Peter pressed his eyes tightly shut and shook his head.

That was when Oliver turned on Lola. "What the *hell* have you done to him?" He spat at her, his voice suddenly high-pitched in fury. "Are you trying to kill us all, is that what you're trying to do? What are you trying to prove, you stupid bitch? What are you trying to *prove?*" And all at once he was violently shaking her, snarling like an animal.

Peter had never seen such an open expression of terror and helplessness cross Lola's face. Oliver was much stronger, he could easily pitch her over the edge. "Oh, Oliver, go away!" he cried out. "Go away, go away!"

And finally Blossom came, plodding laboriously toward them, her cheeks sagging and her mouth pinched, her filthy dress hanging on her like a shroud. "Really, Lola," she began, turning slightly from side to side, her hands behind her back. "Honestly, Lola, I didn't *really* mean those things I said about ruining everything you did; I just wanted to see if saying something like that would make the machine work. To see if you were right. And you *were* right." The oddly persuasive quality her voice had once had, though she was obviously trying to make use of it now, was all but lost under a feeble, ingratiating whine. "And I told the others the truth, I told them I changed what you said, and I promise I won't do anything like that ever again, Lola, if you'll please just come back. Please?"

"Then how the hell do you expect to get the machine to work, if you're not going to do anything like that again?" Lola asked her. "You know that's what it wants; you just admitted I was right about it."

"Uh . . . well, uh, yes, I know." Blossom bit her lips in concentration. "But, you know, Lola," she continued quickly, after a pause, "that doesn't mean I have to do it against *you*. We could do things to the others. Not to you, Peter, of course." She flashed him a quick, frightened smile. "But to the others, to Abigail and Oliver. Especially to Oliver, Lola, you know he deserves it. I know you don't like it that the machine wants us to do mean things to each other, but if it's to somebody like Oliver. . . . Do you know what he said, after he came back from talking to you? He said you—"

122

"Look," Lola interrupted. "There's no point in going on. I'm not going to fall for your crap, and we're not going to come down. You might as well stop wasting your breath."

"But," said Blossom, her fists clenched at her sides and her face growing red and puffy, "but you've *got* to come back. Oh, please, please, I'm begging you to come back. How can you be so cruel? We've got to eat, Lola, please, we've got to eat, we've just—"

"Stop it!" Lola said shakily. "Stop it and get away, just get out of here! Didn't you hear me? We're not coming, it's no good. We're *not coming!*"

Blossom gasped back a sob and stared blankly for a moment, tears clinging to her cheeks. And then strength seemed to return to her and she wiped her tears quickly away, glaring at Lola with her little sparkling eyes. "All right," she said hoarsely. "All right. I gave you your chance to come back. And now you've lost it, both of you! I know we'll get that machine to work without you. And when it does, don't think we'll give you a scrap. We'll let you starve." Her voice dropped menacingly. "And that's not all we'll do. That's not all. You know what the machine wants, don't you? Well," she stopped to take a deep breath, then went on very slowly, "well, you're the ones who are going to get it." And she turned and hurried away without looking back.

It was hardest when the whispers came, and the colored light, which, even as high as they were, flashed brilliantly on the shining surfaces all around them. They would close their eyes and hold their ears and hum, trying to obliterate the precious signals, the infinitely compelling messages commanding them to dance, causing their muscles to twitch; and telling them: *Food, food, the smell of it and*

*the taste of it and the feel of it in their mouths and going
down to their stomachs, the emptiness and the pain in
their stomachs, the pain in their stomachs, the intolerable
pain.*

It helped a bit to hide from the signals, but just knowing that they were going on around them was enough to
create a wrenching agony in them both, a feeling that they
were literally being torn apart. It was almost impossible
not to move—as they both often found themselves doing
—not to jump to their feet and start toward the light, their
arms and legs moving helplessly in the familiar patterns
of the dance. But they would scream at each other to
stop; they would pull at each other, gasping and sobbing,
back up to their high landing, back up to the landing to
close their eyes and hold their ears and crouch, sweating
and shaking, begging for the light and the voices to stop;
and wondering if next time they would have the strength
the resist them.

For they were growing weak. Lola never ran anymore,
not only because she felt too listless and exhausted most
of the time, but also because she was afraid of what might
happen if she found herself alone, anywhere near the machine, when the light and the voices began. Nor did she
want to leave Peter by himself, for without someone to
cling to it would be too easy to give way.

And at first she was worried about Peter. True, he had
shown great determination and strength by joining with
her, by running from the machine and so far resisting its
commands; by turning from Oliver. But he was even less
accustomed to bearing such burdens than she was, and,
along with everything else, his dream world pulled at him
seductively. Going back to the machine meant going back

to the magic room as well, and she was afraid that as their situation grew worse, the power of the room would grow stronger.

Lola could tell when he sank into his daze, his face loosening; and at first she had debated with herself whether or not to try to wake him up. For wouldn't it be easier for him to sit through the terrible relentless commands if he were unconscious of them? She soon learned, however, that it really made no difference. He was in the daze once when the signals started, and within a few seconds, he was struggling right along with her.

"But how come you never seemed to notice them before?" she asked him when it was over. "How come it always took Oliver so long to wake you up?"

"It's . . . hard to explain," he said. "I never really thought about it till now. But somehow, I *do* know what's going on, even when I'm in the magic room, and now I just come right out. But. . . ." He looked away from her, "But when Oliver was there, I couldn't come out until he . . . until he talked to me like that."

At first she had been angry, thinking of all the time that had been wasted while Oliver tried to wake him up, when all along Peter could perfectly well have come out of it on his own. But he kept trying to explain to her that it really wasn't that simple, that it hadn't been so easy, and in the end she had to forgive him. It was too tiring to stay angry.

Nevertheless, she was now all the more determined to keep him out of his trances. And so, whenever he started to slip away, she would shake him, even hit him when necessary. And this was partially successful, because she could always get him out.

But he kept going back. Obviously, the room provided him with pleasure and comfort that he could not resist. If only she could find something even more pleasurable that would entice him to stay out! Rewarding him, she realized, would be more effective than just punishing him. But she had nothing to reward him with except herself. The only thing she could think of at first was the food from the machine that was constantly on their minds; but that, of course, was not available to her.

But she refused to give up. Her hatred of the machine and, to her surprise, her concern for Peter, were too strong. She began going over in her mind everything Peter had done; and she realized that some kind of intangible reward really did exist, if only she could find it. Whatever it was had already helped him do several remarkable things: walk up the stairs alone to find her, break out of the dance himself and push her out of it, and resist Oliver. But what was it?

When she finally saw what it was she felt like a fool for not having known it all along. It was several things, all connected. It was the reward of winning over the machine, which he hated and feared; it was the reward of feeling strong and independent, of having his own identity, a feeling he had never known; it was the reward of caring about her, of being essential to her plan and not letting her down; it was even the reward of her caring about him. In certain ways it was the same reward that moved her, but Peter, being weaker, needed to be reminded more. And so she began to remind him—but not all the time. For something inside her knew—though she was not really aware of it or of where the idea had come from—that the reward would only work if it was given at just the right time.

"Remember, Peter," she would say, whenever he had remained out of a trance for a certain length of time. "Remember fighting the machine. We're winning now, because of you. Remember how you felt after you climbed those steps, how strong you felt. You are strong, Peter. Remember it was you who got me to stop dancing. Without you it wouldn't have worked. I need you. I need your strength. And we're going to win, Peter. We're going to win; but only if you stay out of that room."

Whenever he had just come out of a trance she would turn coldly away and not speak to him at all, even when he begged for the words. She would reward him, not for coming out, but for *staying* out. And instinctively, without really thinking about it, as time went on she gradually lengthened the period he had to stay out before she would speak.

When it began to work, when the trances began to grow fewer and farther apart, then she rejoiced, with the little strength she had for it. And as the trances grew less, Peter's eyes began to take on a new expression, as though they had never really been open before. And at last he came out of a trance by himself, so quickly that she didn't even have time to shake him, and, spontaneously, she embraced him. She had never embraced anyone before.

And so she reassured him at the right times, and rejoiced in his change. And gradually his mind grew stronger as his body weakened.

And hour by hour, the hunger grew more terrible.

And then, how long after Blossom had left them they could not tell, the worst part began.

They had expected the others to keep coming back. They had dreaded it, trying to prepare themselves for more pleading from Abigail, more violence from Oliver, and more groveling and threats from Blossom. They had expected them to come back together, they had expected fights, and they had expected to be dragged down the stairs.

"Go limp," Lola said. "Just go limp when they grab you, then they won't be able to get us down there, they're just as weak as we are."

But strangely enough, no one came. As the endless hours, and then what seemed like days, dragged by, they began to long for the sight of one of the others on the stairs below. At first what they wanted was simply relief from the enervating boredom; but as more time went on, and still no one appeared, their minds filled with uneasy questions that soon began to torment them.

Why weren't they coming up? They couldn't have died of starvation so soon, and yet if they were hungry they certainly would be up here trying to get them to go back. Did it mean they had found some way to get food? Had the machine decided to work without Lola and Peter, or was there a new source other than the machine? Had Blossom and Oliver killed Abigail to eat her? Lola didn't doubt that, in the extremes of hunger, they would be capable of it. All they'd have to do would be to push her off the landing. . . .

But there was another thought, the most likely possibility and the worst of all. Perhaps they weren't here anymore. Perhaps whoever had put them here had come and taken the three of them away, and Lola and Peter were alone among the stairs, starving needlessly.

And it was this thought that finally brought them back down. "Just to look," Lola insisted. "Not to stay or give in.

Just to see what those bastards are up to." And Peter nodded miserably, wondering if this was the end of their plan, and they had failed.

It took much longer than they remembered, for they were weaker now, and their unsteady legs had lost the feel of the stairs. Lola's sense of direction too was stale from disuse, and they took many wrong flights. Nevertheless, as they drew nearer their progress became more direct, for something began to guide them. At first it was faint and they noticed it only subliminally; but gradually it grew stronger and more tantalizing until they were conscious of nothing else, and their feet followed it automatically.

"W-Wait," Peter said when they were very near, grabbing Lola's shoulder. "It's . . . it's food, I smell food. Maybe we shouldn't, shouldn't get any closer."

"We've got to," Lola said. "We've got to get closer and not touch the filthy stuff and find out what the hell is going on."

Finally they reached a stairway from which they could look down and see the whole landing: the colored screen that pulled at them even without flashing, and the three familiar figures, each sitting on a different stairway.

And they were eating, but there was something different about it now. They were shoving the food down faster and more frantically than even Blossom ever had; and as they ate, each of them kept his eyes fastened so tensely on the other two that at first none of them even noticed Peter and Lola.

Lola's knees almost gave way and she swallowed dryly at the sight of those pellets, and the rich fragrance. She didn't trust herself to speak, and Peter was silent beside her; but the others caught sight of them as soon as they had finished eating.

"Look!" Blossom cried out, and pointed up at them, swallowing. Her face was round and pink again, and saliva dripped from her glistening lips. "Look who's here!"

A sudden shadow crossed Abigail's face, as though she were both embarrassed and about to cry, and Lola noticed an ugly bruise on her forehead. Oliver grinned. "Oh, so you've given up, have you?" he called to them. "We knew you would."

Peter couldn't help it. "How . . . how did you get it?" he stammered. "Where did it come from?"

"From the machine!" Blossom cried triumphantly. "From the machine! It works without you now, just like I said it would. We don't need you anymore. Go ahead and starve!"

Lola was holding herself stiffly, her mouth clamped shut. "But . . . ," said Peter. "But how . . . ?"

"Don't know how, Pete," Oliver sang out, chuckling. But his voice was strained and too loud, and the chuckle was more like a cough. "Don't know how or why. But it works. Want to come back? You can if you want to, you know." He shook his head mock-seriously, clucking his teeth. There were black spaces where several were now missing. "You both look kind of thin and pale. Not taking good care of yourselves. You need some fattening up. We'll let them come back, won't we?"

"Well, I don't know about Lola . . . ," Blossom said.

"Oh, sure," Oliver said genially. "Let 'em both come back, even though we don't need them. We can afford to be generous. On one condition, that is." He paused for a moment, and his eyes were suspicious and hard. "On one condition. We don't want anybody interfering with the machine. If you want to come back, you'll have to follow the rules, like we do."

"Oh, cut the . . . ," Lola began, and then her voice trailed off. She was staring down at the slot in the landing. Peter could hardly believe it. Was she thinking of giving in?

Blossom's mouth curled up; Oliver's grin widened. Peter couldn't bear to see her humiliated in front of them. And at any moment the light and the voices might start, and then they would be helpless. There was only one thing to do, and he grabbed Lola and spun her around.

As they stumbled together up the steps, Blossom's voice floated harshly up to them. "You were right, Lola, you were right about what it wants us to do, you knew all along. But it doesn't care who we do it to, you know. And we're running out of things to do to each other. It won't do any good to starve yourselves, it won't make any difference now." Her voice grew fainter behind them. "All it means is you'll be hungrier and weaker when we come. And we'll be coming soon. Very soon. . . ."

chapter 18

For Blossom, Abigail, and Oliver, the hunger hadn't lasted very long at all. Their successful new pattern had begun, in fact, just after Blossom had returned from her visit to Peter and Lola.

Oliver and Abigail, sitting on different stairways, had been waiting for her rather hopelessly. After all, if they had failed, then certainly Blossom wouldn't be able to do any good. Oliver had decided that their next move would be to go up there all together and just drag them down. It was three against two, and he was stronger than either of them. It would have been easier if they had ropes to tie them with, but however they did it, sitting on them or tying their feet together with his pants or whatever, they would just have to keep them down on the landing until the light and the voices began.

Oliver was sure that if that happened, they wouldn't be able to keep from dancing. The three of them, even though they knew it wouldn't do any good, had been dancing frantically every time the signals went on; it was as inevitable as if they were puppets being pulled by strings, and they were helpless against it. If they could only get Peter and Lola down there, and keep them from running away, then they would be just as helpless, and they would dance, and there would be food.

Blossom was about thirty feet away when the lights and voices began. It was amazing, Oliver noticed as he began to dance, how fast someone as fat as she was could move; she practically flowed down the stairs and was into her little path around the hole by the middle of the first repetition. And at the end of the second, a pellet rolled out.

They were too well trained by this time to be able to stop and grab for it, though each of them longed to; for mixed with their relief was the anxiety that this fortunate fluke of the machine would not last. They needn't have worried. The pellets rolled out for a good long time, and when they did stop there was enough, not to satisfy them, of course, for that it never did, but enough at least so that all three of them could alleviate in part the physical pain, and feel warmth in their stomachs once again.

"But why?" Oliver asked, swallowing his last piece. "We've got to figure out why it happened, so we can make it happen again."

"I don't understand," said Blossom, who was hungrily eyeing the five pellets still in Abigail's lap. Blossom always finished first, and Abigail had the annoying habit of eating very slowly, so that she usually still had food when everyone else was through.

"Maybe it was something you did," Oliver said. "What did you do up there, what did you say to them?"

Blossom gazed upward in thought, letting her fingers

play with her lips. "Well . . . first I just asked them to come down, I practically *begged* them." Her eyes slid over to Oliver for a moment, then away. "But no, they were too stupid and stubborn to pay any attention. So then I got mad, and I said we would get the machine to work. . . . Oh, isn't it wonderful! Oh, it feels so good to eat! Do you think it will work again?"

"That's what I'm trying to find out. Go on, what else did you say?"

"Well, I said we would get the machine to work, without them, and that we would let them starve. And now we can!" She clapped her hands together in spontaneous, excited anticipation. "And you know Lola thinks the machine wants us to hurt each other, so I said we'd do mean things to *them* to make the machine give us food."

"Good girl, Blossom!" said Oliver, beaming, and he stepped over to her and grasped her shoulder affectionately. "Good girl."

"What do you mean?" Abigail asked, looking rather frightened. "I don't know what you mean."

"It's very simple," Oliver said in a patronizing voice, returning to his place beside her. "Very simple." How wonderful it felt to be the smart one, the one with the ideas, the one in command! How wonderful to be rid of Lola and that horrible inadequate feeling she always gave him. He even felt strong enough now to be able to say, "Because Lola *was* right, in her dumb hysterical way. The machine *does* want us to hurt each other. For the last four times it's only worked when somebody made someone else feel rotten. It wants us to do that so much that it's even letting us get away with doing the dance without them. At last we really understand. Now we know what to do, and we don't have to worry about being hungry ever again."

Abigail clutched his arm. "But . . . but how can you be so calm, and so . . . so happy about it? Doesn't it scare you? What's going to happen, what kind of things are we going to have to do?"

"You'll find out soon enough," said Oliver, winking at Blossom. "Blossom's already good at it, and I can learn quick." Suddenly his voice was very serious. "And you will too, Abigail; you will too."

That was when it had begun, and there were so many possibilities just among the three of them that Peter and Lola were practically forgotten. Oliver, eager to test his ability to satisfy the machine, got off to a good start by taking Abigail right upstairs and kissing her. As soon as she really seemed to be getting lost in it, he stepped suddenly away from her and told her exactly how he felt. "I always hate you after I've kissed you. All I want is to get away from you, because you disgust me. The only time I can stand you is when I want to do it again. And if there was any other halfway bearable girl around I'd probably be with her instead of you."

The light and voices hadn't started immediately, as they had the last four times, but Oliver hadn't worried, because he knew it wasn't the machine's way to let them tell it when to work. Those last times it had only been teaching them; and now that they had learned, it would continue to perform as randomly as ever, as long as they kept on doing what it wanted. He understood perfectly. Not until several hours after his episode with Abigail did the lights and the voices come on; but the food, even with just the three of them dancing, was more plentiful than ever.

Blossom tried next, and again Abigail was the victim. It was just after they had been fed and, as usual, Blossom had finished while Abigail still had quite a substantial pile. Suddenly realizing that the machine would actually *like* it if she did what she was so desperately longing to do, Blossom stood up, pretended briefly that she was simply wandering around, and then suddenly pounced on Abigail, scooped up everything she had left, and stuffed it into her mouth.

"But you can't do that!" cried Abigail, leaping up. "Give them back! You can't do that!"

Blossom backed away, mumbling something unintelligible through her bulging cheeks, and Oliver grabbed Abigail's wrist sharply and pulled her back to the step. "Now, now," Oliver said, squeezing her wrist and smiling at her. "Temper, temper, Abigail. It's your own fault for eating so slow."

And it was not long before Abigail, inevitably, began doing her fair share. She felt so hungry and wretched that it had been a real blow when Blossom had taken away her food, and for the first time in her life she began holding a grudge. All day the resentment and anger grew inside her. All she could think about was how to get back at Blossom, and at last an idea came to her. When the others had fallen asleep, she got up and moved very quietly over to where Blossom lay on her stairway, her mouth open, snoring slightly. Abigail bent over and as gently as possible began tearing off the bottom ruffle of her skirt.

She had reached the third ruffle when Blossom shifted, wiped her nose vaguely, grunted, and sat up. Then she shrieked. "Hey! What are you *doing?*" she wailed. "My dress, what have you done to my dress, you . . . ?" In an instant she was on her feet, her hands around Abigail's neck, shaking her.

Abigail tried to push her away, but Blossom was surprisingly strong. "Oliver!" Abigail gasped. "Oliver, help me!"

But all Oliver did was rock back and forth on his step and laugh. Indeed, Blossom was quite a ludicrous sight, her face red and puffy, her teeth clenched, and her skirt hanging in loops and tatters from her hips, exposing her huge, jellylike thighs.

Of course Blossom did not soon forget Abigail's act. And Abigail soon learned to be extra careful at meals. There was no longer any orderly dividing up of the food. They would grab what they could get at the end of each dance, guarding it closely and keeping their eyes on the others as they ate.

They also explored the exciting possibilities of two against one. It was no longer very easy for one of them to grab another's food, for they were all guarding it so carefully now; but when both Blossom and Oliver attacked Abigail together, for example, each could get a substantially larger quantity than when trying it alone. Oliver and Abigail could then attack Blossom immediately afterwards; Oliver would get even more and Abigail could get back part of her share.

And as time went on they became interested in more elaborate plotting. Oliver began it by arranging with Blossom that she would hide herself above a particular landing at a certain time, pretending to Abigail that she was going to the toilet. He then very tenderly brought Abigail up to the landing, taking back what he had said before and telling her he really did care for her after all.

And Abigail, though hardly dumb enough to believe him, nevertheless could not resist the chance for even a tiny morsel of affection, though she knew it would probably result in pain. And it did. Tender at first, he quickly became just as nasty as before; and while he was berating her, Blossom, who had been looking on the whole time, appeared, giggling as she watched Abigail's humiliation.

"She'll believe anything I tell her," Oliver said, beginning to laugh along with Blossom as Abigail hid her face in shame. "She'll believe anything. Whenever I want her I just give her some romantic crap and she falls for it every time." Blossom was laughing so hard by now that tears were rolling down her cheeks.

But Abigail was growing tougher, there was no alternative, and as soon as she had gotten over her embarrassment, she began her own arrangement with Blossom. She did not wait until they were alone, but began whispering and giggling with Blossom in front of Oliver, and when he demanded to know what they were saying she merely blushed and looked down. She kept it up for quite awhile, Oliver stiffly pretending to ignore them whenever he was able to control himself, and futilely resorting to violence when he was not.

Blossom went along with it gleefully, both of them watching him out of the corners of their eyes as they snickered together. Finally Oliver, in a rage, ran up to the toilet, and when he returned they were crouching above the landing, on a stairway from which they could see him clearly but were hidden from below. He looked around for awhile, obviously confused, calling their names. Abigail waited for a few minutes, doing her best to keep herself and Blossom from giving themselves away by laughing; and then, at a moment when Oliver's back was turned, simply dropped her shoe down onto the landing.

His reaction was even better than they had expected: With a terrified squeal he leaped into the air and was half-way up a stairway before he noticed their shrieks of laughter and turned around to see the harmless shoe lying there. He raced back and heaved the shoe out into the void, cursing; but it was well worth it to Abigail because from that point on she could drive him instantly into a rage simply by glancing over at Blossom, smiling, and making a remark like, "Remember how high he jumped? Lola must have been right about him after all."

That little trick of hiding above and dropping something on an unwary person, or persons, below, worked a few more times, in various combinations. Oliver once threw *his* shoe with all the force he could manage down at Abigail, making a bruise on her forehead that lasted for many days; and another time he urinated down on both of them, to their intense disgust. But soon this particular device lost its savor, for they all became conscious of it, and looked above them frequently whenever anyone was missing, too wary to be surprised.

And gradually something much deeper than just a tendency to trick and humiliate began to develop in all three of them. It was a total mistrust, an incessant wariness, like the constant expectation of a blow. They would flinch, both physically and mentally, whenever anyone approached, instantly planning a defense. When alone, they would be extrasensitive to even the slightest sound or movement, prepared to shield themselves. But it was not simply being afraid, for aggression was just as important as self-protection, and they learned to detect quickly whenever anyone was in a vulnerable position, and then strike accordingly; to seek out and make use of any weak points. They no longer saw one another as people, but only as things to make use of. And, though there were many brief alliances due to the effectiveness of two against one, they nevertheless became more and more distant from one another. Any sign of closeness or affection, after all, only led inevitably to rejection and betrayal, and it was necessary to keep oneself as invulnerable as possible, to avoid exposing any soft spots. They regarded one another constantly with hard, glittering eyes, their faces expressionless, their movements sudden and furtive. And the more careful they became, the more difficult it became to find ways of hurting each other.

And that was when Peter and Lola made their pitiful little trip down to the landing.

chapter 19

"We'll be coming soon, very soon . . . ," Blossom called after the two thin, stumbling figures, and then, with growing excitement, turned back to Abigail and Oliver. "How could we have forgotten about them?" she asked in amazement. "How *could* we?"

"I guess we were just too involved in what we were doing to think about anything else," Oliver said thoughtfully. "Gee, weren't they skinny, though? Peter looked almost like a different person. He kind of acted different too."

"But don't you realize what this means?" Blossom went on, her eyes shining voraciously. "It's been getting kind of hard to think of things to do; but now, when I start thinking about what we could do to them, a million ideas come to my mind all at once. It's fantastic!"

"But," said Abigail, with what was perhaps the last vestige of compassion left in her, "but maybe it isn't fair." She thought of their gaunt faces and of how unsteadily they had stood, swaying slightly, on the steps. "They seemed so weak, and they . . . they don't understand, they don't know how to protect themselves, they're not *in* it the way we—"

Oliver stood up and slapped her hard across the face, leaving the red imprint of five fingers on her cheek. "Oh, you make me *sick!*" he said. "You and your goody-goody namby-pamby phony slush! What the hell else are we going to do? Now that we've thought of it, do you think there's any way we can*not* start working on them? I'll bet you anything you won't be able to resist."

And it was true. Once they began making plans, Abigail was just as much a part of it as the others. Giggling together as they tried to think of the cruelest ways to go about it was so deeply satisfying in some basic, almost physical, way, that Abigail was drawn into it whether she liked it or not. And, as it happened, she did like it. That final trace of human feeling had escaped from her like the last puff of gas from a sinking balloon.

They began simply, saving for last what they knew would be the most effective trick of all. As soon as their plans were made, they hurried up the stairs to hide on a landing just above Lola and Peter's.

The two of them sat silently across from one another, absolutely motionless. They might have been two pieces of sculpture. Their noses and cheekbones had grown sharp and prominent as the flesh had melted away; their faces were triangular and skull-like, with deep, hollow sockets for the eyes.

Strangely enough, though he was just sitting there, it was obvious that Peter wasn't in a trance—his eyes were alert and he was holding himself erect. They wondered at this change in him, especially Oliver, who somehow didn't like it. And then Peter's thin mouth moved, and he reached out slowly to touch Lola on the shoulder with a long, skeletal hand. "What are you thinking about?" he asked her, in the choked whisper of an aged person.

She did not answer for quite a long time, while the three hiding above exchanged excited glances, their hands pressed against their mouths to stifle the giggles that were threatening to give them away.

Slowly Lola's mouth opened, just a crack. "It didn't take Blossom very long to get fat again," she whispered hoarsely. "I think she might be even fatter than before."

"Mmmm," said Peter, nodding so slightly that it was barely noticeable. And they lapsed into silence again.

Even in her weakened state, Lola still had the power to infuriate Blossom. And it was Blossom who made the first move, taking off her one remaining shoe, a hard little white plastic number that had long since lost its shine, and flinging it down at Lola's head.

It is bad enough when something falls near you unexpectedly from above; it is even more shocking and unpleasant when it hits you on the head, digging sharply and painfully into your scalp. Nevertheless, to Blossom's disappointment, Lola's reaction was surprisingly mild. For a long moment she didn't even seem to feel it (although Peter started slightly). Then she put her hand to the spot where it had hit her, and with a little cry bent her head down (they could see every bone in her neck). One hand still on her head, she picked up the shoe, examined it, tossed it over the edge, and said, "They've started. Be ready for anything, Pete."

Unfortunately, Blossom's shoe had been the only thing

they had left to throw, for they had used every other loose object on each other. And, though Oliver had planned to urinate down on them, he was too embarrassed to do so in front of the two girls. So, quite dissatisfied, they went on to the second part of their plan.

Though the three of them were covered with superficial scratches and bruises, they had avoided any really serious physical violence; to cripple or maim, though it would have been extremely satisfying, would have rendered the victim incapable of dancing, and the dance was still necessary. But Peter and Lola were not. This part of the plan had filled them with special glee, for they felt keenly the restriction of protecting one another's bodies; and, though Blossom was beginning to be nervous about being so far away from the machine, they made their way down to the landing with more excitement than they had felt in days.

Oliver arrived first, Blossom and Abigail close behind. Peter and Lola were bent over, and pressed their faces into their knees. "Hey, Pete," Oliver said. "Don't you even want to say hello? How're you doing, friend?"

Instinctively Peter looked up to greet him. "Watch it!" Lola hissed, and just in time Peter bent over again, so that Oliver's kick merely glanced off the top of his head instead of hitting him full in the face. In fact, since Oliver was barefoot, it hurt him more than it did Peter, which only served to enrage him.

"Stay out of my way, you bitch!" he shouted at Lola, and socked her in the ribs. It made a hollow thump, and knocked Lola to the side a bit, but she did not respond in any other way.

Blossom grabbed hold of Lola's hair and tried to pull her head back, while Oliver, grunting, continued to pummel her on the back and sides. Abigail was left to deal with Peter by herself. She was not accustomed to hitting people, but she knew that it was necessary, and so she began, timidly at first but with increasing force, to pound his head and shoulders with her fists.

But it was so frustrating the way they insisted on staying bent over like that, keeping hidden all the soft and vulnerable spots like their stomachs and their faces. If only they could get at those places, then they would really be able to hurt them. Blossom pulled harder at Lola's hair, puffing, her tongue pressed between her lips, hard enough so that some of it came out in her hand; Abigail began prying Peter's head away from his knees, scratching violently at his forehead with her long nails. Oliver darted from one to the other, shaking and pinching them, trying to roll them over on their backs. And Peter and Lola crouched and gritted their teeth; but they were weak, and began to give way.

But suddenly the colored light was flashing at them, and the whispers were in the air. Almost before the signals had started, it seemed, Blossom, Abigail, and Oliver were speeding down the stairs, too quickly gone to be able to witness Peter and Lola's real agony—though it was an agony that was rapidly losing its sting.

The machine fed them well this time, almost as if it was rewarding them, or else helping them to prepare for the third, and what they knew would be the most effective, part of their plan. For the agreement that they should stop the purely physical attacks and go on to something else was unanimous and unspoken; not only was it no fun to beat Peter and Lola when they didn't seem to mind it much, but it was hard work, and actually painful to them, their only weapons being their own hands and feet. The third part did not have this drawback, and furthermore was absolutely foolproof: There was no way that Peter and Lola would be able to protect themselves.

The difficulty, of course, was saving some of the food, and Blossom found it particularly trying. But since they had been well fed this time there was more food than usual, and the plan was so enticing that when she concentrated on it even Blossom was able to keep a good number of pellets in her hand instead of stuffing them into her mouth. But they started quickly, not trusting their willpower to last very long, and also hoping—for it could just as easily be in two minutes or five hours—to get finished before the machine should start again.

"Oh, why did they have to go so far away?" Blossom whined as they mounted the steps for the second time that day. "If they were closer we wouldn't have to worry about missing the machine."

"Yes," Oliver agreed, "we'll have to bring them down sometime. But after we've been up there a few more times, they'll learn they can't get away from us no matter where they are, and it'll be easier to get them to come down. They may even do it on their own."

"Do you think they'll starve to death?" Abigail asked with a nervous giggle. She was always nervous now, and, oddly enough, unlike the other two, she was still as thin as ever.

"But if they died we wouldn't be able to do things to them anymore," said Blossom. "And they might start to stink."

"Don't be ridiculous," Oliver said in the bossy, pompous voice he was beginning to use more and more. "They'll never go that far. They'll come crawling back to us first, and we can spit at them and watch them grovel."

"But they're getting pret-ty skinny," said Abigail, trying to sound irritatingly whimsical. She knew Oliver hated being contradicted. "Pret-ty skinny."

Oliver stopped in midflight, turned and grabbed the back of her neck, pressing his fingers hard into the soft spots. "Shut up!" he said between his teeth, shaking her. "Shut up, shut up, shut up!" But Abigail kept her mouth in a mocking half-smile, until his hand grew tired and he was forced to let go. "Who gives a shit what you think, anyway?" he said, and started up again. "Come on, we're in a hurry."

Peter and Lola must have heard them approach, for they were back in their crouching positions when they reached the landing. "You don't have to do that, you know. We're not going to hit you," Oliver said.

"And we're not going to throw anything at you, either," Blossom added.

Peter and Lola did not speak or change their positions. The others had expected this, and knew what to do. Blossom began at once, kneeling beside Lola and bringing forth one pellet from the pile in her left hand. She held it as close as she could to Lola's buried nose. "Smell something?" she asked her. "Smell something familiar, Lola? Something good?" She rolled the pellet along Lola's fingers. "Feel something? Has kind of a nice feel, doesn't it? If you licked your finger now you might even get a little *taste* of—"

Lola's movement was sudden, but Blossom was prepared, and the machine had taught her to be quick. In an instant she was on her feet, out of Lola's reach, barely feeling Lola's hand brush against her skirt in its wild grab. For a moment Lola's arm remained outstretched, trembling slightly. Staring into Lola's haggard face with its sunken eyes, Blossom brought the pellet to her own mouth, slipped it in, and very, very slowly and thoroughly she chewed and swallowed it. "Mmmm," she sighed, still watching Lola's eyes. "That was delicious."

Now Peter was looking up at them too. "Want one, Pete?" said Oliver, stepping toward him and reaching out his hand. Holding the pellet between his forefinger and his thumb he waved it slowly back and forth just in front of Peter's eyes. And helplessly, Peter grabbed too.

"Uh, uh, uh, Petey boy," Oliver said as he jumped back, clucking his tongue against his teeth and shaking his head. "Naughty boy, naugh-ty, naugh-ty." He began to chew the pellet, slowly, as Blossom had, and then opened his mouth and stuck out his tongue, with its glob of reddish-brown goo and strands of glistening saliva.

Blossom was still playing with Lola. Desolately, Lola had watched her eat, and then retreated back into her crouch, too weak, it seemed, to be able both to protect herself and be aware of what was happening to Peter too. And Blossom approached her again, and brought a tantalizing pellet once more to her nose, and giggled as Lola, her reflexes slowed, uncontrollably and futilely reached for it another time. More even than denying her the food, it was the beautiful humiliation, the sight of Lola as her absolutely helpless, pitiful victim, that was so deliciously satisfying; of everything in the world, Blossom could think of nothing that Lola would hate more.

They left soon after the pellets were gone, pulled by their ever-present awareness of the waiting machine. Oliver's parting gesture was to sail his last pellet past them both. Laughing as they turned away from the sight of Peter and Lola reaching so slowly and feebly and inevitably for the disappearing bit of food, they made their way down the stairs, taking every opportunity to pinch and insult one another as they went.

chapter 20

And at last the moment came when Lola opened her eyes from sleep and knew unquestionably that if she did not eat soon she would die.

It was quite different from just being hungry. Oddly enough the hunger, after the first hellish days, had for the most part disappeared. Water alone seemed to satisfy them. It was only when Oliver, Abigail, and Blossom came up to play their little games that food was once again unbearably tempting; but since they had not allowed Peter or Lola to get any, the feel and taste of it were almost forgotten sensations to them now.

And not only had the hunger seemed to go away, but the call of the machine had begun to wane as well. Once they had managed to resist it for a certain number of times, the inevitability of its control was broken; and, since they had determined that food did not exist for them now anyway, its one reward grew gradually less enticing. And finally, after the others started their painful visits, the significance of the light and the voices changed altogether: For now, while they lasted, Peter and Lola knew they were safe from the others, and at last came to welcome the signals as much as they had dreaded them before.

No, the feeling Lola had at this moment was not hunger; if possible, it was something even deeper and more instinctive. It was the sensation of dying, coupled with the basic, undeniable urge to live. It was as though she were conscious of every cell in her body giving up, changing one by one from living into dead useless tissue and being carried away, until at last there would be nothing left. The drive to fight this process was not, like hunger, something she had learned to tolerate in an effort to resist the greater evil of the machine; it was a force she had never been fully conscious of before, and in its sudden emergence her will was powerless before it.

"Peter," she whispered. They rarely spoke now, and when they did it was in the barest of whispers, for what little strength they had left had to be saved for their encounters with the others. "Peter," she said again.

Still reclining, he lifted his head slowly and looked at her.

She did not have the time or the energy to waste words. "I'm dying," she said. "I can feel it. All over."

He nodded. "Yes. I feel it too."

"I can't help it. I must eat. I can't die. I'm going down, if I can make it."

Her words were such a shock to him, so overwhelmingly disappointing, that they were more painful than anything the others had done. He even managed to sit up. "No," he said. "Lola, don't give up now. Think of the machine, what it did to them. What it will do to you."

But she was already dragging herself to her feet, using

the nearest stairway for support. "You don't understand," she gasped, pushing herself away and standing unsteadily. "There's nothing I can do. This thing inside me won't let me die. It won't let me."

If he'd had the strength, Peter would have cried out in despair. He would have pulled her down and forced her to stay. But as it was, all he could do was stare at her and gulp two or three times. He knew the feeling she had; his body was perhaps weakening even faster than hers. But his instinct to live was not so strong. For three years his life had been so listless and so empty that there was really nothing to make him hold onto it now. Fighting the machine, in fact, was the only thing that had interested him since the time of Jasper. He did not want to give up the fight just to hold onto the dull emptiness he knew as life.

But as Lola stared back at him, he knew that he would have to go with her. Even though something in her had just broken, he understood that she still hated the machine at least as much as he did, and would always continue to. If he did not give in, and let himself die, she would know for the rest of her life that success had been possible, and that she had let herself fail. Whatever was going to happen to her in the future, it would be far worse for her if she had to bear the failure alone. And he realized that even more important than the fight against the machine was his caring for her. He could not desert her.

He struggled to his feet, trying to ignore the agonizing disappointment. "I . . . I . . . you're right," he said, reverting back to his stutter in the sudden confusion of thinking up his lie. It was a lie he would have to live with from now on, and it had to be said the right way. "I feel it too. Something inside . . . it won't let me die. It . . . it doesn't care about the machine."

"Yes," said Lola, watching him; and then she turned and started down.

Fortunately, it was well before they reached the others that they heard the whirring above them, and looked up to see the elevator coming down to take them away.

epilogue

Of course it took Lola and Peter a long time to recuperate, being fed gently through rubber tubes inserted into their arms; but nevertheless Dr. Lawrence waited until they were quite strong, keeping all five of them in separate hospital rooms and allowing no one to answer any questions.

When at last he felt they were ready, each of them was led through the hushed white corridors, uncomfortably aware of curious eyes turning to watch them pass. What they were not aware of was that one whole wall of the laboratory to which they were taken was a one-way viewing wall, and that behind it dozens of doctors and scientists—and several others—fell silent and leaned forward eagerly as the five of them were led into the room.

They were shocked, at first, by one another's appearances. They remembered gaunt features, broken black fingernails, matted hair, tattered, crusted clothes, and pungent body odors. The shining, combed, and starched people they saw were almost like strangers. Especially to Lola and Peter, for they were not accustomed to the behavior of the other three: their tense, slightly crouching posture; the way their eyes slid constantly from side to side; their quick, furtive gestures—when Abigail brushed back her hair it was not a luxuriant movement as it once had been, but quick and businesslike, as though to keep the hand poised for something more important.

And Peter was different too, though not like the others. The way he stood so straight, and calmly looked people in the eye, and smiled so openly when he saw her, made Lola feel a sudden glow of pride and affection. The two of them hurried together, and briefly clasped hands.

Oliver's first response on seeing Abigail was to slap her across the face; she grabbed his hand and bit it. Then, suddenly remembering the doctor's presence, they stepped apart rather sheepishly. But Dr. Lawrence didn't seem surprised; his only reaction was a slight movement of his lip, and a brief shift of his eyes toward the viewing wall.

"Well?" said Lola, her hands on her hips and her head turning to look around the room. One side of the white laboratory was a vast instrument panel, consisting mostly of video screens, but with a few rows of buttons and little gauges. Lola began to study the screens; and then, almost simultaneously, they all noticed what was on them, and felt such a curious and intense mixture of horror and nostalgia that Abigail even cried out. There was nothing on the screens but stairs.

"Oh, yes," said the doctor, noticing their reaction and moving toward the panel. "Perhaps you are surprised that there are so many video screens, but we really had no idea where you might go if you ever did leave the reinforcement center, and of course had to be prepared to view and record everything. Watch." He pressed a button; there was a flash on one of the central screens, and then there were Lola and Peter crouching, while three demented and disheveled creatures attacked them ferociously, sweating and grunting with exertion.

"Stop!" Abigail cried out, hiding her eyes. "Stop it, stop it, please!"

"Of course, of course," the doctor said quickly, and suddenly the people were gone, and the screen showed only its empty section of stair.

"But why?" Peter said. "Why did you do it? What were you trying to prove? My God, it's so. . . ." He turned to Lola, shaking his head in disbelief.

"I don't know why you're so surprised," Lola said. She gestured at the screens. "None of that is any filthier than all the crap he's already put us through. Let him keep on having his fun with us now, showing off his sick little games. You and I can take it, anyway."

"Yes," the doctor said, staring at Lola. Those behind the viewing wall who knew him were accustomed to the doctor's habitual lack of facial expression, and his cool, well-modulated voice that never rose. But now they were startled by his expression and the tone of his voice. "Because you could both take it, a great scientific project has been something of a failure."

Peter and Lola were watching each other. Lola knew that their secret, the secret that they had been about to give in when the elevator had come, was safe. And Peter knew that his own secret was safer still.

The doctor looked at the blank wall. "In the end, since we couldn't just let you starve, and since we knew we had been quite successful with the others, we decided to move in and take all of you out, and just hope for more consistent results next time. That is," now talking directly to the viewing wall, the doctor removed his glasses and began fondling them nervously. "That is, if we are given another chance." He paused, returned his glasses to his nose, and went on more quickly. "It must be realized that such severe and undetected abnormalities in certain of the subjects chosen is not something that we or our techniques can be held responsible—" Suddenly, he stopped.

It seemed quite strange to the five in the laboratory with him that the doctor kept looking at the wall. They did not realize that the explanation was not for them at all, but directed at those in the observation room; and that they were merely being used as exhibits.

"I should explain that conditioning," the doctor said, "is the means by which any organism learns how to interact with the world in the most effective way, most basically avoiding pain and approaching pleasure. What conditioning essentially consists of is finding out that a certain action on your part will produce a certain response from something else. You learn that if you respond to a specific outside stimulus in a certain way, then you will bring about a specific result. You learn to tell the difference—to discriminate—between stimuli, *if there is a reason to do so.* You learn, automatically, to do the right thing at the right time in order to get the right result: You are *reinforced* to behave the way you do by the results you achieve. People have been studying these patterns of conditioned behavior for years, and we may soon know that everything one does in life can be explained in this way."

Once again he paused. "Now," he went on, "I would like to explain how each element in our project relates to conditioning behavior. To begin with, the stairs."

"Wait a minute," Lola said. "I want to get this straight. You were trying to condition us, right? You were trying to create certain patterns in us?"

"Of course," said the doctor, turning to her impatiently.

"But why were you trying to condition us to do those . . . those things, those horrible—"

Dr. Lawrence put up his hand. "Please let me finish. No one will be able to understand until I have explained each element. Now, the stairs. They served a very important function. In order to achieve the fastest and strongest results, I felt that the reinforcing element—the food—had to be as powerful as possible." He looked at the wall again. "It was essential for the food to be the *only* thing that wasn't unpleasant. If everything else is terrifying, alien, and uncomfortable, how much more intensely gratifying, and necessary, the one pleasurable element will be."

"But you're wrong," Lola said.

"What?" The doctor turned toward her.

"You were wrong. The reward is more important."

"I don't know what you're talking about."

Lola sighed. "It's what you were just saying, about how making everything unpleasant and horrible helped to condition us. You didn't need to. It's the reward, or the reinforcing element, whatever you call it, that really counts. Punishment doesn't work very well. In fact . . . in fact, you might have had better luck if you hadn't used so much punishment, and more of a reward."

For a moment the doctor just stared at her. "How do you know anything whatsoever about it?" he said at last.

Lola shrugged, trying not to look at Peter, who was staring at her as with some sudden revelation. "I . . . I just know," Lola said, and looked down.

The doctor snorted. "Do not interrupt," he said coldly.

"Now, the light and the voices," he went on. "They, of course, were the discriminative stimuli. The subjects learned quickly that then and only then would food be given, depending on how they behaved. As to what the voices actually said. . . ." He moved to the instrument panel and pushed another button, watching them. The voices that suddenly filled the room were closer now, and they realized that they were nothing but blurred nonsense syllables, not real words at all. He stopped them quickly. "That was just a little side issue, actually, to see how each of you would interpret them, and how it would relate to your later behavior. And as for the light. . . ." This time the button brought to life a glowing panel. "Would you mind telling me what color that is?"

Oddly enough, they all hesitated before answering. At last Oliver said, "I think . . . green?"

"No, it's red, of course!" Abigail quickly contradicted him. "But no," she went on. "Maybe not, maybe it could be. . . ."

"It's just the color of the light," said Blossom. "It's not red or green, it's just the color of the light."

"Yes," said the doctor, turning it off. "Well, for your information, you would all have called it red before the experiment. And it is red." He turned back to the wall. "That was to demonstrate how one does not discriminate between colors, or anything else, unless it is necessary; unless the discrimination is reinforced. In this case it was *not* reinforced, the subjects knew it made no difference what color the light was, and soon stopped noticing it."

"But . . . but will we ever learn to tell the difference between red and green again?" Abigail asked in a frightened voice.

"Now, the dance," the doctor continued, ignoring her question. "Although the behavior I hoped eventually to elicit was altogether different, the dance nevertheless served its own very important function. From it, you learned many things: that you would have to behave in a certain way in order to eat, that you would *all* have to do it, that food would only come at certain times over which you had no control, that the things you must do to get it would change, and that you would be instructed *how* to change the behavior, if you were alert enough to notice."

"But if we *all* had to dance to make it work," Oliver couldn't help asking, "then how come it started working with just the three of us?"

This time the doctor didn't seem to mind answering. "That was an attempt to get those two to give in. We felt that if the others were actually eating, and tempting them with food, as we hoped, then they would be more likely to surrender."

"Okay," said Blossom, "but how come sometimes the machine didn't work when the light and the voices were on, even though we were doing everything right?"

"Yes," said the others, stepping closer to him. This was something that had puzzled and frustrated them all.

"You won't understand, but that was what we call variable-ratio reinforcement," the doctor said. "It produces more stable and long-lasting behavior than consistent reinforcement."

As they puzzled over this statement, the doctor went on. "Now, to explain the goal that was the objective of all our controlled conditioning. One of the great problems of the human race is that the conditioning most people receive from life, from the real world, is unplanned—haphazard and accidental. Is it surprising then that people are only rarely well adjusted? That only rarely do they find themselves in a life situation for which their conditioning has prepared them? No wonder that so many people are frustrated and dissatisfied (if not worse), and therefore do not perform with maximum efficiency. Our eventual goal is, of course, to be able to provide scientifically planned conditioning for everyone; but in this, our first real effort with human subjects, our aim was simply to produce a group of people who would be particularly well suited to carry out certain very important jobs."

"Hey, now wait a minute," Lola said. "I don't get it. *Jobs?* I mean . . . what the hell kind of jobs do you need *monsters* for?"

The doctor ignored her. "Our great President," he said, his eyes on the viewing wall again, "has long known the direction of our research, and a little over a year ago I had the honor of meeting with him personally. He asked me if I could provide for him a group of young people, an elite corps, who would be able to follow unquestioningly any order given to them, no matter how . . . uh . . . distasteful or unnecessary it might at first seem; and who, furthermore, would be so cautious and so alert that they would be very unlikely ever to be interrupted, or . . . well, to get caught. If you think about it for a moment, you can see how vital such a special corps would be in missions relating to our international security, intelligence, and defense, as well as certain domestic issues. Not to mention its use in providing directors of concentration camps, prisons, as well as excellent interrogators. And I told our President that yes, I was quite confident that I could provide him with such a group. The funds for such an important project were, of course, quite generous; generous enough to allow for the construction of an environment large enough for the increased operation we foresaw. And then these five extremely fortunate young people were chosen to be the first participants in this historic project. It is too bad that some of them did not realize quite how fortunate they were."

"Fortunate?" Lola said. "You call it fortunate to be put through that hell? And for your information, if you think that my goal in life is to go mucking around in dirty political—"

"Be quiet!" The doctor's voice was sharp, his irritation so uncharacteristically apparent that his acquaintances behind the viewing wall were again surprised. "Your attitude is deplorable," he went on severely. "But eventually we will have techniques sophisticated enough to deal with individuals even as intractable as you. No," and his eyes rested steadily on the viewing wall, "no, I did not come up with five usable individuals, as I had hoped, but it cannot be held against me. This is the first experiment of its kind, after all; one hundred per cent success on the first try is an unreasonable demand. You can see that two of the subjects were incorrigible—no one else, I can assure you, would have been able to deal with them any better than I. And the other three are exactly what we need," and he threw out his arm toward Blossom, Abigail, and Oliver.

Now it was clear to the five in the laboratory that the doctor was very upset, if not actually deranged. Why did he keep talking to that blank wall? And those watching from behind the wall were now even more shocked, shifting in their seats and glancing nervously at one another. Lawrence had never behaved this way before; something must really be wrong.

"I have come up with three perfect specimens," the doctor was saying. "And all five of them can be studied. We will soon learn to be one hundred per cent successful; we will learn from our mistakes; no one else now is as experienced as we are. This project *must* remain in our hands. The three of them standing here are perfectly usable, they will make excellent operatives. In only a few months' time I am sure they can begin their—"

"You mean we're going to keep on *being* like this?" Abigail burst out, unable to control herself. "Isn't it going to go *away?*"

The doctor took a deep breath and nervously adjusted his glasses. "I hope not, but as yet I cannot say for sure," he said stiffly, as though it annoyed him not to have the answer to everything. "This is the first project of its kind, so of course we have no extinction curves. Charts, you know, showing how long the behavior lasts after it is no longer reinforced, and if, in fact, it ever really does stop. That is what we will now begin learning from you."

They were walking in the hospital grounds. Blossom, Abigail, and Oliver did not seem very comfortable being out of doors. Their bodies were tense, and their eyes moved constantly up to the sky and then from side to side. And though they were huddled together in a little group, they rigidly kept from touching one another. They did not smile.

They were between tests. Lola and Peter, they had just learned, were soon to be sent away. "To an island," the doctor had announced, "where misfits are kept." The other three had more tests to go through, and then were to begin their training. What the training specifically was to be, none of them knew.

Lola and Peter were walking behind, watching the others curiously. Suddenly, Oliver spun around. "Stop staring at us!" he said.

"We weren't staring," said Peter, and stopped walking. "We were just—"

"I don't care what you were 'just' doing," Oliver said. "Leave us alone."

Abigail looked terrible, still very thin, with sunken, shadowed eyes.

Blossom was fat, pink, and healthy. "Yes, we don't want you around," she said. "Stop tagging along after us. We don't need you. Get away."

"With pleasure," Lola almost said, but stopped herself. They were pitiful; there was no point in being nasty. "Come on, Pete," she said, and they turned and started in the other direction.

He reached out and took her hand. Neither cared that someone might see. They had been taught all their lives that the only deep feelings between men and women were sexual, but now they knew that it was a lie. They were friends and they loved one another, and their hand-holding was perfectly innocent. It was one more thing to rejoice in, one more way in which they had risen above the system, above the machine. They had won, there was no better feeling than that; and now they were to be sent away. Sent away to a place where people might be like themselves; a place where things would be different, and perhaps better.

"It's too bad about Abigail," Peter said. "She looks so sad, and she was really okay once."

"I know," said Lola. "I wonder what will happen to her. I wonder if that conditioning will ever go away."

"The doctor said no one knows," Peter answered, and they strolled together toward a cluster of stunted trees.

Still in their little group, Blossom, Abigail, and Oliver hurried (they were unable to walk slowly), across the hospital grounds. They stuck closely to the cement wall, feeling safer there. And then the wall came to an end, the path took a sudden turn, and they were face to face with a traffic light—a green, blinking traffic light.

Without hesitation they began to dance.